The
SONG
of
DRAGONS

a novel by

Kathleen Bradford

Book Three of the Gateways Series

Published by Glass Spider Publishing
www.glassspiderpublishing.com
ISBN 978-0-9997070-5-0
Library of Congress Control Number: 2018938919
Cover design by Jane Font
Proofread by Stephanie Simonson

PROLOGUE

He glided through the nets easily, able to locate and move through the small holes and tears. Few were aware of the unique sight his kind possessed, allowing them to see in many directions at once and still be keenly focused on their destination. But he didn't want to think about them, think about *him*. Mr. General Cornelius Haft. *Ha!* The man was lost, and who knew if he'd ever find his way?

Not thinking about him, Sabastian! he scolded himself. His heart was too filled with joy and excitement. They were coming! And he couldn't wait to tell Lixten.

He moved stealthily through the yard, keeping an eye out for the birds, even though there weren't but a couple still flying around these days. Still, he had to be careful. *You never know what crazy thought the General might have and decide to call on them just for giggles... Not thinking about him, Sabastian! Not! Too happy, yes.* He moved carefully from rocks and posts, camouflaging himself to match each as he went. *Another secret Cornelius doesn't know*, he thought smugly, buzzing a chuckle to himself. *Not!* he scolded himself again.

When he reached the large concrete building, he nestled up against the outside steel frame and hopped up to the barred rooftop. When he saw that there was no one around, he quickly flew in, landing on the tail of his friend. It still saddened him to see that, where the spikes at the tip were once bright and sharp as razors, they were now cut and pummeled to blunt bone. His bright indigo and orange colors had faded and dulled to gray and putrid brown.

On a soft sigh, he flew up and up until he reached the massive head of Lixten, the dragon prince, and whispered in his ear. "They're coming, my friend. A guardian is coming."

Lixten shifted, making the thick steel chains attached to the metal collar around his neck rattle.

"What nonsense are you babbling, Sabastian?" he rumbled.

"A guardian, they're coming."

Lixten lowered his head in disappointment. "There is already a guardian here that has done nothing. It has made no difference."

Sabastian fluttered down to be in Lixten's line of sight. "Yes, but this guardian has not been shaped to have no courage, nope. The one that is here lives in fear for himself and for all of us. Fear of what Cornelius would do to you. But he has a secret, Lixten. He does, he does."

"What secret?" Lixten demanded, shifting his body, causing the ground to tremble.

Sabastian flew out of the way, dodging the swing of Lixten's neck. "I cannot say, not my secret, nope."

Lixten moved quickly, spinning his head around to be nose to nose with his tiny friend. "Why have I not seen this secret in his mind? I think you tell me lies, Sabastian."

Sabastian was unaffected by Lixten's hostility and clasped his tiny legs onto one of Lixten's nostrils, staring him in one very large eye.

"You do not talk to him, my prince, do not."

Lixten shook his head, trying to detach Sabastian to no avail, but Sabastian let go willingly and hovered in front of him.

"A guardian is coming. They are brave and they are strong. There is hope, there is," he told his friend eagerly and began to fly in circles above Lixten's head, singing off key. "Hope, hope, yes, yes, there is hope."

A small flicker of light sparked in Lixten, but he quickly extinguished it. The memory of defeat echoed through his body in a heavy sigh.

"I have succumbed to the General, Sabastian. Too many lives were already lost, and there is no going back. There is no more fight in me. I have let my tribe down, and now we are doomed to stay here until the Winged Gods take us home."

Sabastian said nothing and bowed his head. He knew Lixten's dismaying mood was partly from the grief he was feeling for the loss of his mate. The last breeding cycle went horribly wrong, and Lixten blamed himself. When he told Sabastian of the tragedy, Sabastian thought he had lost his friend for good. Lixten had let his emotions free and truly cared for Ari. So when Cornelius came to take the eggs away from her, she fought him. Lixten tried to intervene, but Cornelius mistook his intentions and slayed Ari for what he interpreted as a threat and defiance from Lixten, then took his eggs anyway, to be raised as beasts without love or the teaching of their ways.

Lixten's thoughts mirrored the memory, and anger bubbled inside him. It had been years since he'd longed for the fire. He had become nothing: without strength, without honor. He was here only to serve as a breeding tool for Cornelius. He sighed deeply again, resigning to his fate, circled and fell onto his side, causing the ground to tremble once more.

"Tell me a story, Sabastian."

Sabastian pushed his sadness away. He was not so willing to give up hope, so for now, he only nodded and rested on Lixten's head. "Of course, Your Majesty."

Lixten ignored the title, closed his eyes, and just listened to the soothing tone of Sabastian's voice as he took him into a world of escape and dreams.

"There was a great queen named Namara," Sabastian began. "She had descended from the very highest of realms. Her only intent was to bring peace and happiness to all other realms . . ."

CHAPTER *One*

*S*he soared through the air, her arms outstretched, head back and thighs clutching the smooth, glistening back of her carrier. The warm wind rushed over her body, and she couldn't remember a time when she felt so scared and excited and free all at the same time. She felt the subtle movements of swaying side to side, diving down and then back up again, as she gripped the scales of the neck with both hands and cried out in sheer delight.

Then she heard an angry roar and her body went tense, the delight dissolving into panic. She saw the steel arrow, thick as a tree trunk, graze the neck of her carrier just as he maneuvered a sharp dive. Her hands slipped, and she lost her grip. She was falling. Helpless terror froze her mind, only the sensation of falling . . . falling. She saw the huge wings flapping above her, causing the sunlight to flicker in and out of her eyes.

Then she saw the open sky, the brilliant colors of blue and soft orange, the silhouettes of the dragons dancing above her as she fell. She closed her eyes, and a peace filled her heart, and in that moment, she completely accepted and embraced her fate. Then she felt the large talon wrap around her body, plucking her from the air.

When Valeen opened her eyes, she blinked in the sunbeams that shone through the gaps of the drawn curtains in her bedroom. The vague memory of the utter terror and absolute peace she'd felt in her dream was being replaced by an acceptance that she was back in her own bed. But still there was a disappointment in the fogginess of waking up. *When did these dreams become so okay with you, Val?* she wondered.

Then the scent of coffee brewing tickled her nose, awakening all her senses at once. She heard the birds singing outside her window and muffled voices coming from the living room. A quiet groan of pleasure escaped her throat. *How nice it is to have someone around to wake up to, and, better still, that he makes you coffee.*

"I thought I heard you stirring in here," Luke said, peeking in the doorway.

"I don't think you *heard* anything. You've probably been stalking back and forth for an hour."

Luke didn't deny it; he only grinned. He was a little anxious about their upcoming adventure, and impatiently waiting for Valeen to wake up. "I made you coffee."

"Yeah, the nose knows."

Luke scowled and sat on the edge of the bed. "What?"

Val closed her eyes, stretched, and flopped her arms out on the bed. "Never mind. I'll get up and shower. Have you heard from Ian or Laura yet?"

"No, not yet, but it's early. You could call them when you're out of the shower."

The eagerness in Luke's voice made her chuckle. "I will, just give me a few minutes to wake all the way up."

Luke took one of her outstretched hands and brought it to his lips, softly kissing the back of her wrist. "Good morning."

Valeen rolled onto her side, cupping both of her hands around his. "Good morning. What's for breakfast?"

Luke smiled and kissed her forehead. He slapped her on the butt, got up abruptly, and headed for the kitchen. "I'll throw something together. Now get up. We have some traveling to do."

Valeen rolled onto her back, her arms still stretched out. "Fine, I'm going, I'm going. When was the last time you were there, anyway?"

Luke stopped in the doorway and thought about it for a minute. "Oh, I don't know, I guess I was just a boy. Now get up. Let's be on our way already." He turned around, holding on to the doorjamb. "Are you sure you're all right with traveling again?"

"Yes, I'll be fine. Now go. We have to eat, and I have to call Laura."

Luke tapped the side of the door. "Okay, if you're sure."

Val stood and tossed a pillow at him. "Would you get out of here? You're wasting time."

Luke ducked the pillow and left.

Shaking her head, Val rushed to the shower, dismissing Luke's question completely as she stepped into the warm water. It didn't matter anymore—well, it didn't matter today. She was sure she could handle the trip through the gateway. After everything she had seen and experienced in the last year and a half, she thought nothing could surprise her any longer. Most of her fear and doubts were becoming more like hesitant anticipation of new discoveries—a new reality of who she was, what magic existed in this world, in other worlds, and in her. *Other worlds* . . . the idea made her chuckle as she let the warm water of the shower wash over her.

"Are you about finished in there?"

The sound of Luke's voice made her jump, but she laughed anyway. She turned off the water and slid open the curtain. There he was, standing with a steaming cup of coffee in one hand and her towel in the other. The chiseled features and piercing emerald eyes that saw right into her soul were capped with silken black hair he kept tied back with a leather strap. The man could still take her breath away.

She reached for both the coffee and towel at the same time. She took a sip of the coffee first, then handed it back to begin drying herself rigorously. "I was just thinking about our newest upcoming adventure." She wrapped the towel around her, taking the cup from him, sipped, and handed it back again as she began to dress. She was starting to feel a little anxious and excited and afraid all at the same time now that the haziness of sleep was washed away.

"Laura called while you were in the shower. She had some questions about the attire. I set her straight. They were still packing, so we have some time yet. Why don't you sit? Have some breakfast and coffee."

She glanced over to where she had packed for the trip herself weeks ago. "I'm almost ready. What is the *attire*? What did you tell Laura? I only guessed what we might need."

Luke put the mug in her hands, took her by the shoulders, and kissed her on the forehead. "I told her I didn't know what the weather would be like. It's been a while since I was there, but I didn't remember it being a whole lot different than what the weather was like here, so probably still cool." He gently pushed her to sit on the bed. "We are all packed, and then some. I have settled a bit now, and so should you. We still have plenty of time—why don't you sit here for a minute and take some deep breaths—for both of us, before you set something aflame. I'll get us breakfast."

She watched him walk out of the room and began taking deep breaths as he instructed. She wasn't entirely sure that she wouldn't in fact set something on fire . . . or worse. There was still so much to discover. But the terror she'd once felt about her gifts was now just a flicker in her mind. She was more cautious now; it was more of an uncertainty than an absolute denial.

As she breathed, her mind settled and focused on the sounds she'd woken up to. She listened to the birds outside that welcomed the rising sun with their song, the mumbled voices of the TV, and Luke clanging pots and pans in the kitchen. The sounds were calming and comforting, and she sat there just breathing it all in.

They cleaned up the breakfast dishes, both starting to feel a little restless again, but each for a very different reason. Val imagined Luke was feeling like a kid going to an amusement park, and she was feeling . . . well . . . a little terrified as the reality of their next adventure began to sink in.

She filled her cup and went out to her back porch. It had become a routine to starting her morning. She would clear her mind and set her intentions for the day. Laura had once told her she could tell when Val had missed a morning of quiet time. Even though Laura was her friend and loved her, it was enough to keep up with the actual events that took place in her world; it was something else entirely to keep up with what would start circling in Val's head when she started to spew everything out.

"I still love you, but go be quiet somewhere and come back," she remembered Laura telling her.

A very large dragonfly zipped in front her and stopped. It was close enough she could see the dark green eyes and translucent wings fluttering. Its humming buzz and direct stare were hypnotic in the quiet of the morning.

You are the guardian? They are the guardian?

It was a sound like a tiny whisper, just a small tingling inside her head. *Was it saying something to me . . . ?*

The screen door opened and slammed shut, startling her, and the dragonfly flew away into the woods. Puzzled, she followed its path until it disappeared, then turned around to see Laura step out, carrying a backpack.

"Well, think of the devil."

Laura let the backpack fall off her shoulder. "Why were you thinking evil thoughts about me?"

Val smiled and hugged her friend. "I wasn't. Is this all you brought?" She gestured to the backpack.

"No, Ian has the rest. I can't tell if he's excited or worried. This is new for him, you know?"

"It's new for you too," Val told her dryly.

"Yeah, well, I've known you longer, and I trust you."

Val looked at her sideways. "It's new for me as well, you realize?"

"Yes, but it will be fun. Besides, I'm mostly curious. Aren't you?"

Valeen stuffed her hands in her back pockets and stared out into the forest. "I suppose 'curious' is one word for it."

Luke and Ian came out, bags and backpacks slung over their shoulders. Val took hers and took one deep breath.

"Okay, let's get this show on the road, before one of us changes our mind."

"Not a chance," Laura said, and headed for the forest. Ian and Luke shared a glance and then followed.

***

Laura scowled at the entrance to the gateway, the excitement and curiosity shifting to uncertainty and a little fear. "Val, we're sure about this, right?"

Val chewed on her lower lip and looked at the entrance. It shimmered in the morning sun rays that shone through the trees, welcoming them to walk through. "Well, no, actually, I'm not."

Laura's mouth dropped open. "You don't know how to play this game very well. You're supposed to be unafraid and reassuring." She turned to Ian. "Maybe we should reevaluate our vacation choice."

Ian took her hand and pulled her closer to him to peck a kiss on her temple. "I'm sure it will be fine. Luke and Val would never put us in danger." He glanced at Luke for support. "Right?"

Luke gave them a short nod and took a deep breath as he approached the doorway. "Well, not intentionally." He hitched his backpack onto his shoulder and took Val's hand. "We should be on our way. I haven't been there in a while; it could have changed a bit."

Ian looked at Laura, covering his own uneasiness. "You're right, they don't know to play this game."

Valeen chuckled and reached out for Laura. "Just take my hand and think about dragons. Don't let go," she added fervently.

Laura squeezed Val's hand. "Don't *you* let go. Or you," she said, glancing back at Ian.

Ian brought their joined hands up to his mouth and kissed the back of Laura's wrist. "Not a chance."

Val was touched by the gesture, and it settled her. She took a deep breath and exhaled. "Okay, Mr. Music, lead the way."

"What?"

"Never mind, let's just go."

Luke shook his head, dismissing the reference, and stepped through the gateway. Linked by clutching hands, the others followed.

***

Cornelius stepped out of the concrete building, his son Tobias following quickly.

"Nica is almost ready for mating, but she needs some taming yet. See to it today, Tobias. I want her ready by month's end."

Tobias stared at his feet. "Shouldn't we wait until Lixten is feeling . . . better?" he asked Cornelius meekly, then remembered how Cornelius felt about his questioning and abruptly looked up at his father, erasing any sign of emotion from his face.

"I mean, he might still be a bit hostile since the last cycle, and we wouldn't want a good healthy female killed by a hostile dragon." Tobias thought quickly, speaking without any sign of fear even though he shook on the inside. He had trained himself to be like one of Cornelius's soldiers. That was what his father expected of him, and any sign of emotion was just not allowed. Not since his mother died.

Cornelius stopped and studied him, searching for any sign of weakness or defiance. Tobias was his best trainer, had a way with the dragons, *like his mother*. He let the thought go when the rage and despair started to bubble inside him, dismissing the idea completely. He had a job to do and had molded Tobias into the kind of soldier he needed to succeed. The high committees counted on him to maintain an order and provide a strong, nonthreatening, and confined species. The details of how he accomplished that service were not of importance. Tobias was right; he couldn't afford to lose a healthy female.

"Do what you do, and we'll see how Lixten behaves in the next few weeks," he ordered.

Tobias nodded. "I'll see to it, sir," he responded like any good soldier, and turned on his heel and headed for Nica's lair, where Cornelius kept the other young dragons.

Nica was the only female besides Mara and Areve. Mara was completely unapproachable with the idea of breeding, and Areve, well, Areve was just unavailable. Tobias had told Cornelius Mara was incapable of producing offspring, but it was important to keep her alive for training of other females. In reality, Tobias was afraid for her life. If given the chance, she would try to eat Cornelius. And that would be bad for all of them.

A thought occurred to Cornelius, and he hollered for Tobias.

"How much longer before the younger males are ready to stud?"

Tobias was far enough away from his father that Cornelius didn't see the cringe of his body or the clenching of his teeth, and he avoided giving a definitive answer.

"I will check on them later today," he replied obediently and turned away.

Cornelius knew the risk. He hadn't seen Lixten so defiant in years. He had to punish him; he didn't have a choice. His men and all the realms could be in danger if he didn't show his power and put a stop to any aggression Lixten showed. The very real possibility that the dragon prince could reunite his clan was a risk he couldn't take. That was why he kept them separated. Areve, the Queen Mother, as Tobias explained to him, was considered the mother of all the offspring. But she was lost to them since the slaying of her mate, Rem; she'd withdrawn so deeply no one could get through to her. But at Tobias's behest he kept her alive. There was still a connection of some such kind that kept the beasts connected and alive. In Tobias's way, he had convinced Areve to at least eat, so Cornelius didn't have her disposed of. He didn't understand any of the mumbo-jumbo Tobias sputtered, but the boy did have an insight, and Cornelius would use it as long it served him.

On a disgusted sigh, he headed for his house. He had guests coming and needed to prepare. The idea of having strangers visit disturbed him greatly. He didn't need outsiders coming to observe his domain. He'd made this place and taken control in the way he saw fit. He didn't need anyone coming in and questioning his methods. He reported to the higher-ups of the realms, none of whom asked how he did it; they just wanted to know that their realms were safe from the beasts that would torment their people and slay their livestock.

But deep down he knew that if he refused any visitors, it would raise suspicion, and the higher-ups might think he didn't really have any control and rethink his position. No, he would welcome his guests, one of whom he'd heard had great magic, so he would have to conceal a lot of what he did on a daily basis and put it off for a few days. Try to keep them out of restricted areas and only allow them to see what he wanted to them to see. He would use Pip to keep them occupied and keep an eye on their whereabouts at all times.

It's only for a few days. I can manage. And what of this man with 'great magic'—what could he do? This place is mine to rule, and besides, dragons have no magic of their own. They are beasts, mindless beasts that do as they are trained. The problem before was they had no training. They were feral and had no one to govern them. Now they do.

16

"Pip!" Cornelius yelled as he entered his home, hitting the button that controlled the mechanical steel doors with more force than necessary.

Pip stumbled into the foyer, appearing from what seemed to be nowhere. "Yes, sir?"

Pip was only a couple of years younger than Tobias and fiercely loyal to Cornelius, since Cornelius had taken him in when his father was killed in the great battle when they first arrived here. Pip was sure Cornelius shared more of his private thoughts with him than he did with Tobias, and one day he would replace Tobias's posts. He would learn all he needed from Cornelius about the savage beasts and one day even take Cornelius's place as ruler. The thoughts tasted sour in Pip's mouth, and his stomach churned. *Is it the idea that I would have to go outside?*

A voice at the back of his mind spoke. *No, you love Tobias. Betrayal is not in your heart, Pip . . .*

"Pip, are you listening to me?" Cornelius barked. "We have guests arriving. Prepare one of the larger rooms on the third floor."

Pip dismissed the feelings and shoved them deep inside. "Yes, sir," he answered with a short bow and hurried up the stairs.

"And Pip—I want to you serve them as you serve me. They are not allowed in restricted areas. You will see to them at all times."

Pip didn't really understand the order; he didn't know of any restricted areas. But he knew how Cornelius felt about guests and agreed.

"Yes, sir." He nodded and continued up the stairway.

CHAPTER *Two*

When Luke stepped out of the gateway any cheer or excitement he may have felt seeped out of him as he looked around at his surroundings.

"What in all the hells?"

Valeen was looking back over her shoulder, pulling Laura and Ian behind her, causing her to bump into Luke's back. Luke's troubled words didn't register at first.

"What? What's wrong, Luke?"

When she turned to see what had made his whole demeanor shift, her heart broke.

"That was amazing!" Laura was saying to Ian, gripping his arm with both hands in excitement. She all but stumbled into Val, who had also stopped abruptly. She saw the brightness in Ian's eyes fade.

"What is it? Are you hurt?" She felt the dismay coming off of Valeen. Then she turned and looked around at what everyone else was seeing.

There were no birds singing; there were no flowers blooming. There were muddy paths potted with slushy puddles, and in the distance, they could see huge buildings made of concrete and metal beams, with small barred openings that served as windows. Large trucks and tractors were parked in rows on one side of what seemed to be some kind of compound sectioned by wooden fences and barbed wire. On the other side, there were large steel arrow bolts with razor-sharp points stacked neatly next to a contraption that resembled a mechanical catapult. The whole atmosphere was gray and gloomy.

They all stood silent until Laura stepped closer to Valeen, putting her hand on Val's shoulder, leaning to whisper in her ear. "Are we in the right place, Val? Should we go back?"

"I'm not sure. But I think we are," Valeen whispered back over her shoulder and then stepped closer to Luke. "Are we in the right place, Luke?"

Luke said nothing for a minute, just stared, trying to rein in the shock and disappointment. He was in utter disbelief.

"This is not how I remembered it. I'm sorry, we—"

They all turned toward the rumbling sound of an engine, where they saw an oversized golf cart with a single driver who was waving and hollering something none of them could understand. Glancing around at each other with unspoken agreement, they started to walk toward the approaching cart.

Valeen noticed the house in the distance behind the approaching cart. Obviously, that was where he came from. She felt some relief and hope that if they did stay, that was where they would reside, and not in one of the concrete buildings.

As if Luke were reading her thoughts (which wasn't unusual), he turned to her and the others, exhaling some of his disappointment. "I need to know what happened here." His tone was pleaded for consent.

Ian gave him a short nod in understanding. Laura and Val looked at each other, again with unspoken agreement.

"Okay," Val said, and they once again turned to meet their host.

When he pulled up next to them, he shut off the engine. "Welcome to my realm," he said enthusiastically, thrusting a large hairy hand out to Luke. "I am General Cornelius Haft," he announced with authority. "I apologize for the delay in not being here when you first arrived."

He was a big man with shaggy blond hair and icy blue eyes that showed no kindness or welcoming. It was obvious the man was at the very least annoyed by their presence. Val immediately felt like an intruder. She instantly did not like the man. There was something dark and slimy about him.

Luke reluctantly but graciously shook the man's hand, meeting his gaze.

"Thank you for having us. I thought this was the dragons' realm," he said to Cornelius smoothly, masking his disappointment but at the same time challenging him.

Cornelius kept his eyes locked on Luke's for a moment, and the two of them did some kind of male sizing up of each other. Cornelius was the first to break. He barked out a laugh and slapped Luke on the shoulder.

"Of course, of course. We'll get to them later."

Luke wasn't ready to submit so easily. He deliberately kept them where they were standing, not allowing Cornelius to hurry them away. Again as smooth as silk, he pulled Val to him. "This is my wife, Valeen."

Cornelius turned to Val and cupped her hand in both of his; they were cold and hard, and there was no sincerity in the gesture or his words. "It's a pleasure to meet you. And who is this fine couple?" Cornelius hurried on, pulling his gaze off of Val, not waiting for her to reply.

"These are our friends Laura and Ian. They are Natives from the third realm," Luke told him.

"This is their first trip through the gateway, and we're hoping it will be memorable for them," Valeen finished.

"It's nice to meet you, General," Ian said, holding out his hand in that easy, nonthreatening way he had about him.

"Oh, I see," Cornelius said. A glint of disgust flickered across his face, but he quickly covered it and pasted a smile on his face. "The land of the unaware." The insult was not lost on Val, but before it could fully register, he continued, hastily shaking Ian's hand. "Well, Mr. Ian and Miss Laura, I'm glad you could make the trip."

Cornelius turned away from all of them and reached down for one of their bags. "Now, let's get you and your lovely ladies settled." The statement was more commanding than suggestive.

Even though she felt a bit uneasy, the last thing Valeen wanted was a battle of wills from these two men that could easily turn into a fistfight. She truly wanted to make the best of this experience for Ian and Laura. *Maybe the weather will clear up. It could just be the gloom in the air that is shadowing my feelings about this man.* Following Ian's lead, she casually stepped up to Cornelius.

"Thank you so much for having us, General. I'm sure it will be all we expect," she lied—the difference being that she was better at it than Cornelius.

Cornelius glanced at Laura and Ian, deliberately not making eye contact with Luke again. "Of course, my lady. Well, shall we go get you settled?"

"Lead the way," Val said cheerfully and gestured toward the cart.

When Cornelius began to help them load their bags, Val gave Luke a warning glare. He responded by rolling his eyes. Laura snuggled up against Ian, and he wrapped his arm around her shoulders, kissing the top of her head.

They were all quiet again, silently taking in the devastating scene on the short trip to the big house. The air was damp and chilly, a kind of cold that seeped into Val's bones, causing her to shiver. The trees that surrounded the grounds were bare, with spindly dead branches that stuck out at odd angles. The foliage nearer to the ground was dry and brown. There were no signs of new growth or tiny buds about to bloom. It reminded Val of the visions of the uncreated places, but without the life force vibrating in the air waiting to be ignited. This was a dismal place.

As they approached the house, Val noticed the only green anywhere you looked was encircled around the property. The house itself was huge, three stories and a turret with a balcony that looked like it could be used as some kind of lookout. *Luke is right; there is something wrong here. I can feel it.*

She reached out to take Luke's hand and squeezed, giving him a reassuring smile. "We'll figure it out," she whispered to him as they came to a stop in front of the house.

Cornelius was lost in his thoughts. The one with great magic, he assumed, would be a problem. He would have to be very careful and not provoke this man. *This is my realm. I made it. What do these people know of dragons? They never had to do battle with them. They were mindless, vicious beasts.*

"Well, here we are. My house boy has prepared rooms for you on the third floor," he announced without the false cheer in his voice he had before. "I'll get you settled, then I have some things to see to."

Just as they were clambering out of the cart and gathering their bags, the large red door opened, seemingly by itself, and there stood a young boy with short jet-black hair cropped neatly around his face. He wore a red velvet jacket and tan trousers but no shoes. *Interesting,* Val thought. Then she became aware that the green around the house was not grass at all, but painted dirt.

"So where are the dragons? This is their home, isn't it?" Laura blurted out, catching everyone off guard.

At first Val cringed, as everyone stopped what they were doing, stunned into silence. But then she was grateful for the bluntness of her friend and wondered why it had taken so long for Laura to show her colors. She looked into the skeletal trees, hoping to see some kind of color or movement she could point out to her friend, but only saw and felt the eerie dread that hung heavy around them.

At first Cornelius dismissed the question and hefted one of the bags off the cart while gathering his thoughts. "Oh, they're around."

Val glanced at the open door, half expecting to see the young boy come out to assist. But he didn't move from the entrance. Instead an older boy, probably closer to Luke's young friend Sean's age, pushed past him and jogged to the cart, hastily picking up some of their baggage.

"Sorry, I was caught up," he said to all of them, but glanced apologetically toward Cornelius.

Cornelius scowled at the young man. "This is my son, Tobias," he told them, shoving the bag he'd just pulled off the cart into Tobias's arms. "He and Pip will help you carry your things to your rooms." He gestured toward the door where the young boy still stood.

"He doesn't come outside," Tobias offered, answering the unasked question in everyone's mind. Then, with full arms, he headed toward the door, unceremoniously dropping bags at Pip's feet. Pip scrambled to pick them up and followed Tobias into the house.

"Shall we?" Cornelius gestured to the door.

They followed him in and waited in front of a spiral staircase while Cornelius pushed a large metal button on the wall that closed the red door that Val had just realized was made of heavy steel. With a soft clank and sharp click the door closed, and they were locked in. The flicker of hope and excitement she'd had that this place held some kind of magic when the door opened on its own deflated, and her uneasiness turned to a bit of fear as she glanced around at the others, whose expressions mirrored her thoughts. Val thought she saw a sinister grin slit across Cornelius's mouth, but then it was gone.

"It's for our safety," he told them, and began to ascend the stairway without further explanation.

They all followed in silence, climbing the three flights of stairs in single file and then going down a long hallway. Val inspected the interior of the house, taking it all in. She couldn't help herself. The floors were made of wooden planks covered with different kinds of area rugs with no matching colors or themes. There were marble and bronze statues of various soldiers, other mythical creatures, and, of course, dragons. There simply was no rhyme or reason to the décor.

They stopped at a large wooden door with intricate carvings. "This is it," Cornelius announced as he pushed open the door.

When Val stepped into the room, her breath hitched. It was the ugliest room she had ever seen. It was overdecorated with red velvet and gold fringe. The crowded room had a sofa and settee, with a padded footstool, two high-backed chairs, and a small round table with four more chairs encircling it. All were varying shades of red with gold trim. The curtains were made of heavy red velvet, and the walls were papered gold with red stripes. Behind them was a small kitchenette painted gold with red cupboard doors. *Well, I can't unsee this room,* she thought.

"Your sleeping rooms are off to each side." Cornelius pointed.

Luke, having sympathy for the visual assault he knew his wife would be experiencing, stepped up and shook Cornelius's hand. "Thank you,

General, this will be just fine."

Cornelius's chest puffed with pride and a genuine smile started to break through, but it was quickly gone when Pip appeared in the doorway.

"Um, sir."

"What is it, Pip?" Cornelius barked.

"Well, um, sir . . . Master Gordan sent me . . ." Pip's eyes darted around the room at the others, then quickly looked away and down at his feet. "Um, it's Mara, sir . . ."

Both terror and rage ignited in Cornelius's eyes. But before he could get out Tobias's name, the young man came out of one the sleeping rooms and rushed out the door, pushing Pip aside once more.

Cornelius recovered, stuffing any sign of dismay. He turned back to Luke, thrusting a key into his hand. "If there is anything you need, just let Pip here know and he will get it for you." Without further comment, he hurried out.

Pip watched Cornelius retreat, then turned back to the others. "Is there anything I can get for you?"

"I think we're okay for now. Thank you, Pip," Ian told him.

The boy visibly relaxed at Ian's soft-spoken tone. "There is a button on the wall next to the bookshelf. Just push it if you do need something." He pointed to a tall shelf that had only a couple of books on it and two empty tapers. "The nights get chilly, so I'll have some more wood and coal brought up for the sleeping rooms," he told them, and without waiting for a reply, he turned on his heel and was gone, closing the door behind him.

"Well, that was a warm welcoming," Laura said as she tossed her shoulder bag onto a nearby table and put her hands on her hips. "So, which room do you want?"

Val sighed and looked around the room. "We'll take the one on the right, although I am a little terrified to go in."

"Yeah, Cornelius could use a good decorator. Maybe you could put out some subtle hints while we're here," Laura told her.

"I'll go in first," Luke told Val, pecking a kiss on the side of her head. "Just to make sure your senses are not further assaulted." He took a long look around, grinned and shook his head, then went to inspect the room.

Ian began to stroll around the room, poking at the gaudy décor, picking up knickknacks, examining them and then setting them back down. He began thumbing through the books on the shelf.

"These books are all about dragons," he said to no one in particular. Pulling one out, he started skimming through the pages. There were graphic illustrations of dragons yanking small children out of their mothers' arms, or disemboweling men and animals with anguished faces, indicating they were being eaten alive. Some of the pages were of dragons in flight, spitting fire onto burning villages.

Laura walked over to peer over his shoulder. "Oh my God! Do you think they left these in here to scare the hell out of us? Or just to have the information of what the danger is?"

Ian shrugged. "I don't know. Maybe both." He slammed the book shut and placed it back on the shelf. "I'm thinking it's only one version of the truth, though."

Laura glanced over to Valeen, who was staring out the window, distracted. "What do you think happened here, Val?"

Valeen sighed. "I don't know. I am so sorry, Laura. I really wanted to share a magical place with you."

Laura moved next to Val and rested her head on her shoulder. "I'm sure it is a magical place. Maybe we just came in the off-season. And besides, it's still early. The sun may still come out."

"Hey, they left us some spirits."

Val and Laura turned toward Ian, who was holding up a bottle of wine and smiling.

"Where did you get that?" Laura asked excitedly, but a little wary at the same time.

"It was here, in this basket. I missed it with all the other stuff crowded in here." Ian scowled. "It doesn't have a label, but there are four glasses."

"I would let Luke taste it first. They can make some pretty potent stuff out in the universe," Val warned, remembering her experience from just a sip of what she drank at Emery's.

"Taste what?" Luke asked, coming out of the bedroom.

"Apparently, they left us a welcoming gift," Laura replied.

"Yeah, they want us good and drunk so we're not aware of what is going on in this place," Valeen mumbled.

"I don't think Mr. Cornelius would intentionally drug us, Val," Laura said, picking up a glass and thrusting it at Luke. "But you go first."

Luke grinned and took the bottle from Ian, who eagerly handed it over to him.

"So how's the room?" Val asked Luke while he deftly uncorked the bottle and began to fill a glass.

24

"It's not so bad, if you like canopy beds and royal blue more than blood red," he told her, handing her a full glass.

"Canopy beds!" Laura handed her glass to Ian and ran into the other bedroom.

Luke sipped from his glass and sighed. "It's just wine," he told Val and Ian, sounding a little disappointed. "I think we're safe." He handed the bottle back to Ian. "And not a bad one either."

Ian started to fill the glasses when Laura came out, looking somewhat disappointed.

"Val, you really need to leave a business card or something with this man. Our room is emerald green and just as overly stuffed with extravagance."

"Come sit and have some wine, my lovely wife," Ian cooed and held out a glass to her.

Laura went all soft and squishy at the term of endearment—a sight Val was still getting used to seeing in her friend. She took the glass from Ian and sat on the sofa. "It does have a canopy bed, so that's something."

Luke decided he needed to lighten the mood in the room. They all had experienced so much disappointment in just the short time since arriving here.

"Let's have a toast. To what may come, may we be enlightened," he said enthusiastically.

Val sniffed the contents of her glass and sipped, still a bit worried that Luke's tolerance was greater than hers.

"It's fine, my dear, it is only wine. It may be a bit stronger than you're used to, but safe enough."

"Well, cheers, then," Ian said and drained his glass. "It does seem to go down smooth."

Luke raised an eyebrow at him. "You might still want to be careful, though."

Ian shrugged and poured another glass for himself.

CHAPTER *Three*

Tobias ran to Mara's lair. He had to get there before Cornelius. The dragon was obviously already annoyed, and the sight of Cornelius would only agitate her more, which could end badly for Mara.

He heard the shouting of men and the whine of Mara before he entered the building and was even more relieved that it was him and not Cornelius who'd arrived first. There were two workers, one being who Pip referred to as Master Gordan. They were being tossed about while trying to hold on to ropes they had wrapped around Mara's neck. *Fools!* he thought with disgust. *Are they trying to get themselves eaten?*

She was much stronger than just two men, stronger than a hundred men. Out of spite, Tobias just watched the men being tossed around the room as Mara swung her head back and forth, snapping at them in the air.

The only reason Cornelius had the illusion of control was because these beings were proud and stayed true to their word. And the word was, surrender for the good of all. But there was a cost to that surrender. Lixten had made the choice to conform with the expectation that Cornelius would leave if they stopped fighting back. But Cornelius thought he'd found his calling, "the ruler of dragons," and had stayed and built a home here.

Lixten didn't understand the deception, and it didn't take Cornelius long to break the young prince's spirit as he made him witness the senseless slaying of all the young dragons, before they were even a threat. He began a process of creating his own breed of dragon by controlling the mating process and then removing the eggs to be hatched in isolation. Many females were killed when they fought for their young. That was when Lixten abandoned all hope for his kind to ever be free again, and he sent out the order to all that were left. They would no longer fight. They would preserve the lives of those that were to come at all costs.

Rage bubbled inside Tobias, but he stuffed it down as the dragons had done.

"Mara, my beautiful," he said calmly and stepped up to the steel gate.

Mara stopped thrashing and, as quick as a snake, whipped her head around, stopping within inches of Tobias's face.

The men holding the rope lost their grip and tumbled into a wall. They staggered to their feet, relieved. Tobias had a way with the dragons, everyone knew. But it was never clear how. The reasons for it were unspoken; no one dared to admit the possibility that these beasts were intelligent beings or could communicate. That would mean that what happened here and what still happened here was barbaric. And they were the barbarians.

"Leave us," Tobias commanded the men, who left without hesitation.

He gently reached up and removed the ropes from around Mara's neck, tossing them into a corner. He gently caressed the top and side of her head, running his hands softly down her long, slender neck. She was spectacular to look at, even though her lavender and indigo colors were fading. She still held herself with grace and nobility.

"My beautiful Mara, what has you so upset?"

Mara didn't respond at first; she just absorbed the soft and gentle touches from Tobias.

I am heartbroken, Tobias heard her say in his mind.

And what would have you heartbroken, my princess? Tobias thought back to her.

The latch on the door clicked to open. Tobias jumped back, and Mara stood to her full height, her head barely clearing the top of the thirty-foot ceiling, as Cornelius stepped in.

"What is going on? I have guests," he barked.

Tobias searched desperately for an answer Cornelius would accept. That she was heartbroken wouldn't register with him. He didn't see them as intelligent, feeling beings. Then Tobias noticed some loose straw that had been kicked up during her thrashing sticking to her side.

"Perhaps there is some discomfort from the straw poking into her underbelly."

Cornelius studied her from a distance.

Can I eat him today? Tobias heard her say in his mind.

Tobias looked down at his feet to conceal his grin. *No, not today, my beauty.*

Cornelius reached for a broom with a handle the length of three men.

Tobias quickly stepped up to him. "I'll brush her down. You can go see to your guests, sir." He wasn't sure Mara would not in fact eat Cornelius; even if she didn't like the taste of man, she was upset, and dragons made their own decisions. There was no need for bloodshed today.

Cornelius shoved the broom at Tobias. "I have other things to see to. Move her to an outbuilding and change out her bedding," he ordered, and left.

"Yes, sir," Tobias mumbled through gritted teeth when the door clanged shut behind Cornelius. He and Mara looked at each other for a moment.

I miss my sister, Mara told him.

Tobias sighed. *I know. I miss her too. I am so sorry, Mara.* He felt so much guilt and shame he bowed his head, unable to look at Mara any longer.

Mara felt the sadness that ran deep in Tobias. It enraged her. He was a fine young man; he was true and honest, respected and honored their beliefs and traditions—well, as much as he could—and most importantly, he listened to them, heard them. But he was lost in his fear and sorrow. *You should have let me eat him.*

Tobias propped the broom against the wall but still could not bring himself to look at Mara. Instead he began the mindless task of rolling up the ropes.

My beautiful Mara, we both know I could not stop you. And we both know of the vow you agreed to and the chaos it would cause. There will be a day of glory, beautiful Mara," he said, turning to face her. He went to her stall, carelessly unlatching the gate, and began to brush the loose debris from her sides. She began to purr and bask in the pleasure of his kindness.

He would not have to move her to change her bedding; dragons were very clean, and their current living conditions were appalling to them. Mara would happily let him clean out her lair, would even offer instruction on how to do so efficiently. They had always kept their nests clean, would clear out any wet or loose debris several times a day.

Tobias stuffed his fury deep down inside. It would always bubble up whenever he thought too long or hard about the conditions Cornelius had forced them into. It was a place so deep inside himself that not even the dragons could read how he felt. He had his secrets, but it was not time to share them.

He was grateful for the ease of the task. He had to get to the forest. It had been a few days since he'd been able to escape long enough to not be noticed. He also had to check on the other hatchlings and change Lixten's bedding as well.

Lixten made him nervous, though not a frightening nervous. There was no dragon he feared. It was more of an anxious kind of nervous. Lixten never spoke to him. Tobias was certain Lixten did his best to pretend he wasn't even there, and he wasn't entirely sure Lixten even listened to his thoughts. The large dragon seemed to be just as lost and uncertain as he was. And there was no reaching Areve at all, to try asking for assistance. Areve's survival instincts kept her eating and drinking; her body was there, but she was not. It felt like her soul had left but a deeper sense of duty needed her to stay alive for those that remained. *I should be grateful they are still alive. Keeping the bond somewhat thriving.*

"What of our guests?" Tobias spoke out loud and stopped his raking as a glimmer of hope ran up his spine. He shook his head, dismissing the idea immediately. He scooped the last of the old straw into a barrel and stepped out of the pen, remembering to latch the gate. He glanced up at Mara. "Not that it matters."

What is that you say? You know I can't understand that language, Mara scolded.

Feeling her annoyance, Tobias responded in kind. *Sorry, Mara, I was just talking to myself.*

Mara circled and lay down on the fresh bed. *Well, that's a ridiculous thing to do.*

Tobias smiled at her. *I know. I have to go check on the hatchlings now, but I'll come and visit you later, bring you a meal.*

Mara didn't respond, only sighed deeply. Tobias had no more comfort he could give her. She was calm—still sad, but calm, and that was all he could do for her . . . for now. He bid her goodbye and stepped out into the gloom. *It doesn't seem as dreary as it did yesterday,* he thought. *Is there something . . . lighter in the air?*

"That's a ridiculous thought, Tobias, get a hold of yourself," he told himself, then grinned and shook his head, remembering Mara's words. He glanced at the big house. *I wonder . . . ?* But he quickly squashed the thought and went back to his chores.

***

Sabastian let the wind carry him through the air. The subtle, chilly current lifted him higher and higher until he hovered in front of the window to the rooms where Valeen and the others were staying. He knew it was a risk coming this close to the house, but most of the birds had left the realm when the battle stopped and Cornelius set them free. *Nope, nope. No birds here today. Free to fly, free to fly,* he sang to himself.

He wasn't sure how Cornelius had found out about the connection between the dragons and his kind. The man had no magic of his own. Sabastian supposed Tobias could have told him when he was just a boy, still vying for his father's love and attention. *Before Heather had her accident.* The thought made him shudder. He shook his wings as if physically shaking off the memory and focused on the people on the other side of the pane. He wanted to see what their intentions were, if they had a plan. He knew they could help, could save his friend. But did they know it?

As he hovered, he watched intently. He couldn't hear what they were saying, but observed many different gestures and expressions. It always fascinated him how many different emotions these beings could display in a matter of seconds. *I wonder if they even realize that about themselves.* He saw Miss Valeen go through so many in just the short time she stared out the window, looking right past him: first the disappointment, then the sadness, then the acceptance, and then, to Sabastian's delight, the hope. It all happened within just a few moments. *Yes, very interesting indeed. I guess that's what makes them so unpredictable. But I see no fear, no fear at all in her.*

Sabastian maneuvered up and over to get a better look at the others through the window. *No, no fear in any of them. We are saved! Stop. Can't.* He shook his head. *Not too happy too fast. It may annoy Lixten, and an annoyed dragon could squash you like a . . . a bug!* Sabastian chortled at his own joke and couldn't help but do a somersault in the air as he flew toward Lixten's lair.

His mind wandered into the past, when there was the fragrance of flowers in the warm air and leafy green trees with branches that reached for the skies. When there were the bright golden suns that shone down on the realm, catching fractals of light off the wings of the royals as they soared. Sabastian sighed. When was the last time he'd witnessed happiness in this place? *Was it only before Cornelius arrived with his young, pretty wife and infant son? Was there still beauty here? Yes, yes. Sweet Heather, she was beauty.* She tried to keep the happiness, he remembered, and sorrow filled him.

No, no, no. Not remembering. NOT! Too happy. There is no fear in them, no fear. And sweet Tobias, he has his secret. Sabastian's eyes darted around frantically, as if searching for anyone who might be listening to his thoughts. *Shh! It's a secret. Can't tell, can't!*

***

Valeen and the others decided they would explore the house after their meal, and to Valeen's relief, it wasn't all frilly and overdecorated.

Laura had stopped to admire a large tapestry depicting a scene of a place similar to what Val had described in her recent adventure through the gateway to Luke's world. *It was my world once,* she recalled, scowling to herself.

Ian stood in front of a wooden statue—a dragon, of course. Although it stood over seven feet tall, he imagined it was still only a fraction of their actual size. With talons and razor-sharp claws, feathery wings, and a scaled body, it was much like the way they were described as mythical creatures back home.

"Well, I guess they're not mythical. Obviously, someone had to have seen one at some point in our world," he said to no one particular.

It was Luke who responded absently, studying the books on yet another shelf. "Someone more than likely brought the memory with them when they came to your realm. Probably not even aware of where the memory came from."

Valeen gazed out the large bay window. The gloom was darkening, and she could feel that night was approaching. *There is no sun setting, only the grayness of a cloud-covered sky,* she realized. She looked past the painted green dirt and muddy pathways toward the concrete buildings and large equipment, studying the huge razor-sharp bolts, catapults, oversized chains, and thick ropes. The awareness flooded into her like a thick, sticky tar. At first it was disbelief, then nausea, and then the rage that brought tears to her eyes.

"Luke, I know where all the dragons are!"

Before anyone could react to Valeen's outburst, a small, timid voice clearing his throat had them all turning toward the doorway. Pip stood just staring at them, the two parties waiting for the other to respond.

Valeen immediately felt that she should not reveal her thoughts while this young boy was present. She could not identify if it was something she didn't trust in him or an instinct to protect him from the horrors he may not be aware of. She dismissed her feelings and stepped forward. "Do you need something, Pip?"

Pip straightened his shoulders, afraid he might have let them linger too long in the main library. He wasn't entirely sure what "restricted areas" might include as far as Cornelius was concerned. Of course, the General could change his mind from moment to moment, but Pip prided himself on being able to keep up with the whims of the General. *He is a very busy man. He has a lot to take care of. The dragons are untamed and unruly beasts.* "I have arranged evening refreshments for you before you retire for the night. They will be sent to your rooms."

Val nodded cordially to him. "Thank you, Pip, we will be right up."

"Yes, ma'am." Pip bowed, then turned to leave.

"Um, Pip?" Valeen called out.

"Yes, ma'am?"

"These books here." Val pointed toward two very large bookcases. "May I take a couple back to our rooms to read?"

Pip stared at her blankly. No one ever *asked* if they could read the books. Cornelius usually had to force and threaten Tobias to read them for his lessons—which Pip didn't understand either. He loved it when Tobias read to him, and then when he taught him how to read himself.

"Um, I guess it would be okay," he stammered.

Valeen smiled warmly at him. "Thank you, Pip. I promise I'll bring them back when I'm done."

"Yes, ma'am," Pip said, and ran out of the room.

Luke stepped up to Valeen's side and pecked a kiss on her cheek. "There was no reason to frighten the boy," he teased. "Now, what about the whereabouts of the dragons?"

Valeen was staring out the doorway Pip had run off through, trying to pinpoint the discomfort she felt from his presence. *He's just a little boy. How can he be any kind of threat?*

She sighed and filed it away. "Not here. Let's go get our 'evening refreshments.'"

Laura tugged on Ian's hand. "I think the boy scares easily anyway. I am ready for refreshments, and I hope they include a tall glass of wine."

Valeen went to the shelves and selected a couple of books that had caught her eye earlier. "Go ahead and go up. I'm right behind you. I just want to check on something."

CHAPTER *Four*

Pip admired himself in the mirror; he no longer noticed the paleness of his skin, the dark circles under his sunken eyes, or the slightness of his frame. His short black hair laid straight and flat against his head, trimmed like a blade across his brows.

He adjusted the collar of the jacket that was three sizes too big and smoothed out the velvet lapel, letting his fingertips linger over the gold embroidery. This was his father's dress jacket, and he felt proud and strong when he wore it. His father had been killed in the great battle when he was just a toddler.

It didn't matter that he was too terrified to go outside and that there was no place to show off how handsome he looked. There was nothing out there for him anyway. The sun had stopped shining years ago, and the cold dampness in the air made his frail body ache. It was at Heather's insistence that he be raised by her with Tobias. Cornelius would remind him often that it was at his approval that Pip got to stay.

Tobias would go outside with him when he was too afraid. The beast that killed his father was still alive out there. He was chained and submissive, Cornelius assured him. But still the terror of what he had witnessed was too much, and he could not go out alone. Then when Heather fell, Tobias had become withdrawn and distant, leaving Pip alone to fend for himself in his own grief of losing the only mother he'd ever known. And now his fear had become something else, and he could not go out at all anymore.

So he would just stay in his room, drawing or painting other places, other mystical creatures, but never did he draw or paint this place, and never dragons. It didn't matter anyway. The General was too busy to admire any of his work. Pip understood it took a lot to rule a realm and dismissed the General's disinterest. And Tobias was just too full of grief and anger to share them with. So Pip kept his drawings to himself. He hung them on the walls of his room, where he would lie in his bed for hours, daydreaming about visiting those places and seeing the different creatures—the ones he could see in his mind, the ones that were soft and gentle and kind.

He shifted his stance to admire his reflection once more when a thought came to him. *Maybe the General's guests could help me with my little problem and maybe even take me with them when they leave. Just to visit, of course. This is my home.*

He pulled the jacket off and hung it neatly in the back of his chest. *Would the General allow me to leave?* Pip scoffed at the thought. *Of course he would. I am like a son to him.*

Something niggled at the back of his mind, and he felt panic bubble up. He pushed it away, berating himself for acting like a child. *It's nothing. I am just tired, that's all.* And with the thoughts stuffed away, he climbed into bed and dreamt about dragons.

***

"Cornelius is keeping the dragons in those buildings. And according to what I've read so far, not very comfortably, considering their size," Valeen announced suddenly.

Laura and Ian moaned at the thought, and Valeen thought for a moment that Ian might just explode. She had never felt such an intense shift in him before, and it took her by surprise.

"Well, we're going have to do something, aren't we?" he told them through controlled anger.

"I think we need to verify what we're all thinking and find out what happened before we decide to let the General and his minions be set aflame by the dragons," Luke said, trying to contain his own rage and not wanting to believe the other realms would allow such an atrocity.

Laura stood and went to the window, wrapping her arms over her chest for comfort, envisioning the buildings in the darkness. "I think we should start investigating first thing in the morning."

***

Valeen sat up in bed, skimming through one of the books. "It says here that the dragons have a common connection, and when one is in distress or is killed, they all feel it," she halfheartedly said to Luke, who was already drifting into sleep. "If Cornelius has managed to contain them, there would have been some kind of horrible event that took place."

"Mmm hmm" was Luke's only reply.

That was the thought that was keeping her awake—that, and the idea that there weren't many buildings. She laid in the canopied bed, staring into the darkness. The very idea that the dragons were being held captive made her sick to her stomach. *Why would anyone want to keep a being so magnificent caged and hidden?*

Really, Val? Your ancestors did it for hundreds of years to their own people.

Sighing and turning on her side, she gazed out the window into blackness. There were no stars, no moon, only black. *What has happened here? Luke was right; we have to find out. It would go against everything we are to just leave.* She turned onto her back again and thought over the discussion she'd had with Luke and the others while referencing the books she'd taken from the library.

She turned on her other side, this time facing Luke's back. *He probably isn't asleep either.* But she had no words to console him, so she just snuggled up close, breathing him in. It was comforting and soothed her, and she finally began to drift off, dreaming of a great battle filled with terror and anguish.

***

Tobias got up early, before any light began its daily ritual of trying to shine through the gloom. He had to travel quite a distance—to a place that was hidden, where many of the dragons used to live in deep caves and coves. A place Cornelius thought had been deserted long ago.

He picked out an old mare, Rosy. Silently he walked the horse to the edge of the bare trees before he climbed on. He didn't use a saddle. He had worked out a plan that, if Cornelius ever noticed him missing, he could use the excuse that he'd gone after a horse that had wandered off. *If he ever noticed.*

He hefted the large sack over his shoulder with one arm and looped a rope over Rosy's head with the other. It had become an easy ride, as Rosy was now familiar with their occasional journey and knew where they were going.

When he arrived at his destination, he first noticed the shallow cave was bigger, and had been dug deeper into the rock. He felt relief and fear at the same time. Often, he questioned his reasoning for attempting such a blatant defiance. But something inside him could no longer be contained and screamed out for him to do something. And now it was done. There was no turning back. He just didn't know where it would all lead.

He took a deep breath as he slid off Rosy, only to have it hitch in his throat when he spotted the small green bud shooting out of one of the limbs of the tree he was about to tie the rope onto.

"Do you see? Do you see? It's hope, hope, hope! We are saved! My prince is saved!" Sabastian's small voice chattered excitedly.

Tobias jumped. "Sabastian, what are you doing here?"

"I know your secret, you know I know. I am safe. I am stealthy." Sabastian's eyes darted back and forth to emphasize his point. "Did you see? It is color. We are saved!"

"Hush, Sabastian! We don't know what it means. There could have been dozens of green blooms that we have not seen, only to brown and fall before we even noticed. I don't want you riling up Praxton for no reason at all," Tobias gently scolded.

Sabastian lowered his head. "Have not seen color, have not, there is hope," he mumbled.

"Praxton? Praxton, are you here?" Tobias called out in a hushed voice.

There was a rustling of dry branches and dead thorny bushes in front of the cave. "Where else would I be, young master?" a deep but youthful voice answered, and a magnificent-looking dragon emerged. Although he was small in comparison to a full-grown dragon, he still stood a full man's size taller than Tobias. His colors of indigo and fire orange were bright and shocking to the eyes in lieu of what Tobias was used to seeing; even the other hatchlings' colors came in dull and faded. The sight of Praxton's colors took his breath away.

"You have grown—and made your cave larger, I see." Tobias reached up to stroke the smooth, scaled neck of Praxton. "I brought you some food."

"I will have a deep cave before long," Praxton told him with pride. "But it does tire me some."

"Yes, yes. Very nice, very nice. You must eat, must eat. There is hope. Hope," Sabastian chattered as he fluttered around in the cave, inspecting the walls.

Praxton rolled his eyes and swung his tail, deliberately missing Sabastian but still forcing the small dragonfly to zip out of the way. "Why did you have to teach me your language? Now I have to listen to this bug chatter nonsense all the time."

Tobias gave Sabastian a warning glare, then turned to get the sack of food he'd set near the horse. "You would hear him anyway, in your thoughts. Just like I have been teaching you, it is the way your tribe communicates. And that 'bug' is part of the reason your kind still exists." He made sure the rope he'd tied around the tree was secure and stepped up to Praxton. "There are guests at the house, and he's excited."

"Yes! And they are—" Sabastian began.

Tobias gave him another glaring look, and the dragonfly put his nose in the air and continued his inspection of the cave. Tobias dumped the raw meat onto the ground for Praxton. "I apologize for not getting here sooner. The General has had me busy preparing for our visitors."

"It is of no matter," Praxton responded matter-of-factly. "There are wild creatures about. And look, I can make fire." He gestured toward a patch of scorched ground, and then bent down to eat what Tobias brought him.

Tobias's insides turned to jelly. "Praxton, you have to be careful. If Cornelius finds out you're here, we both could be slaughtered."

"I em areful," Praxton said with a full mouth of raw meat. He swallowed thickly. "I am at my best during the night. I see clearly in the darkness." He bent for another bite, again not waiting until he finished chewing to speak. "Ets etter ery ay."

"Praxton, I can't understand you with your mouth full of food," Tobias scolded. "Use your thoughts."

Finding my way in the dark, it gets better every day, Praxton told him, still chewing and slobbering unceremoniously.

Tobias could only stare at him, a bit queasy and a bit fascinated with the pace at which the young dragon ate, then it all clicked together. *That's amazing, Praxton!* he thought excitedly. *I knew some dragons had individual strengths. But I had no idea in which ways.* The answer sprang into his mind from somewhere deep inside him. *You're a night dragon! Wait, how do I know that?*

Praxton swallowed a large chunk of meat. "I knew that. What does it mean?"

Tobias started to pace. "I'm not sure. I'll have to see what I can find out." *I should record this in my journal. What about the other dragons? How many different gifts are there? Maybe I can see into the hatchlings, see what is developing in them. I've never tried probing.* He'd always suspected he could probe the minds of the dragons, was pretty sure they searched his, but thought it to be rude and invasive if he did it. They had been through enough.

He stopped pacing and looked up at Praxton. A stringy piece of bloody meat hung out the side of his mouth while he chomped. "Praxton, we really must work on your table manners," he finally said.

Praxton swallowed. "What do I need a table for? You toss my food onto the ground."

"Yes, yes, ew. Manners," Sabastian added, zipping away as Praxton halfheartedly snapped in the air at him.

Tobias chuckled and shook his head. "You know, Praxton, one of these days you're going to actually hurt him or worse, and you would feel terrible."

Praxton huffed at the thought. "I could, but you have taught me to be precise in my exercises. And I am very precise."

Sabastian buzzed around Tobias's head in quick circles. "You laugh. You laugh. Tobias laughed! We are saved!"

Tobias couldn't help but smile. It had been so long since he'd felt real joy. He was thoroughly enjoying himself and the company he was keeping. "Yes, Praxton, you are very precise."

Maybe it was time he took a risk and approached his guests. He had to tell someone. *Why do I keep those journals if I'm just going to keep the information to myself?* He searched his memory for his reasoning to start keeping record to begin with but couldn't come up with anything; it was more of a calling in his heart to start writing down everything he discovered.

He shrugged the thoughts away, too excited to dwell on what he didn't understand, and began to gather his things and pack them onto Rosy. He said his goodbyes to Praxton. It was difficult to leave him, but he knew it was safer for both of them to keep him hidden. He glanced at the tiny green bud on the tree, and a flicker of hope ignited in his heart. He refused to let it take hold and began the slow ride back to the compound.

He let his thoughts wander as Rosy ambled through the trees. He'd known it was a risk taking Praxton away. He had told Cornelius the egg did not survive without its mother and hidden it under blankets in his room. He would read out loud and talk to the egg every night without knowing why he was so inclined. It was that voice inside him that told him that was what he should do. It was his mother's voice. It had also fascinated him that the egg hatched so quickly. Praxton had come after the other hatchlings, and it took months for them to finally crack. But Praxton hatched in a matter of weeks. It was something else Tobias didn't understand but just went with it, hoping that eventually he would get some clarity.

Maybe it was the type of dragon he is . . . a night dragon? Because you gave him your love . . . Again his mother's words echoed in his heart.

CHAPTER *Five*

Valeen and Luke didn't wait for Laura and Ian to wake, or for anyone to come offer them a guide through the compound. They quietly and casually walked out the front door, determined to find answers. It was still early, but it felt warmer than when they'd first arrived the day before. It was silent: There were no birds singing, no insects humming, not even the sound of crackling ice from the frosty dew that covered the ground and buildings.

"Does the sun ever shine here?" Val asked Luke, searching the sky for any break in the gray cloud cover.

"It used to," he sighed, following her gaze into the sky. "There were actually two suns. I remember it never got fully dark."

Again, Val had no words of comfort for the sadness she heard in his voice. She simply nodded and took his hand as they began their stroll down the muddy paths, avoiding the slushy puddles that had formed in the deep ruts left by the heavy machinery.

When they got to the first building, Luke inspected the large bolted and chained door. It was clearly locked up tight, but he tried pulling it open anyway. They both jumped back when they heard a rustling sound, and the ground beneath them trembled.

"Earthquake?" Val asked.

Then she felt that old familiar spinning in her head. It had been barely noticeable anymore. It was like she had moved into a higher consciousness where the sensation was a normal part of her existence. But this . . . this was different. She heard whispering. She knew it was in her head, but more like it was with Mary—one of the Sun People she'd assisted in getting back from the voids in between realms last summer. She knew Luke was talking to her, but she could only hear the sounds of the whispers that were filled with heartbreaking, pleading anguish echoing through her mind. She saw the concern on Luke's face as he rushed to her side, wrapping his arms around her, catching her as if she were about to fall over. Then the voices started to dissipate. She felt weak in the knees and was glad that Luke was there to catch her.

"Did you hear them?" she asked him.

"Hear what? I just saw the color drain out your face and you begin to fall. Are you okay? What did you hear?"

Val steadied herself but still hung on to Luke as she searched his eyes for any sign of knowing. "The whispers. I couldn't make out what they were saying. They were all talking at the same time." She studied the large door to the building. "It didn't feel like they were talking to me, though. It was a conversation I was only a witness to."

Luke put his arm around her shoulder and led her back toward the house. "I think we need to go get Laura and Ian and find someone to open these bloody doors."

***

In the building set far away from the others, Areve stirred. Something inside her mind sparked, touching her heart. She hadn't allowed herself to connect to any of other dragons on that level in a very long time, had consciously disconnected the cellular thread from fear that her grief was so great it would actually cause more death of her tribe. Her once-brilliant colors of pink and lavender that blended into indigo and ran down her tail into deep purple had faded long ago to almost no color at all. She seemed old and frail, felt weakened and useless. The only reason she could justify not throwing herself onto one those hideous contraptions that horrible human had slain her mate with was because she had a duty to her brood, to her realm.

Who is that who invades my mind? she demanded. There was no answer. *Tobias, is that you?*

She knew the boy brought her food and fresh straw, and had attempted several times to communicate with her, comfort her. He had his own sweet mother's gift. But Areve just could not make herself respond. And then one day he just stopped trying. Like all the rest of them.

She searched the darkness, even though her eyesight, like her color, was fading. Her heart ached for the sky and the suns, for Rem. This was why she went to that dark solitude in her mind. The pain was just too much. Although she fought it, the prickling of light she felt brought her back to an awareness she'd avoided all this time. And the memory flooded in.

The day was warm and sunny, the flowers and trees in full color and leafy bloom. It was a time she felt free and proud as she watched the invasion of the humans through the gateway. She watched intently, camouflaged in the trees as the first ones arrived: the

General, his mate, and their young son. She felt the connection immediately; the gift was in the child but strongest in the female. They were here to talk with them. There was some kind of arrangement to be made. There was a misunderstanding in the other realms.

She really only paid attention when the others started to show up. They started to bring weapons and large equipment in with them. And then the building began. Trees were torn down, and the flowers and grass were stripped away. It was this that prompted Rem to approach the female. He needed to try to communicate directly. The people were destroying their home. The day the female and her child were having some kind of meal on one of the grassy areas still intact was when Rem landed in front her with Sabastian in tow.

Tears ran down Areve's face, splashing onto the dry, dusty straw. She could not make the memories stop. They played on and on in her mind, and a rage she'd let go of long ago began to resurface.

The bolt came out of nowhere, striking Rem in the chest. The terror and shock on his face mirrored the expressions on the female and child. Areve felt the sharp pain in her own chest, and the anguish was devastating to the entire tribe. Her scream echoed through the realms as she took flight and found her target: the man with the contraption. While other soldiers quickly snatched the screaming woman and crying child up and carried them into the house, Areve set her sights on the man who'd let the bolt fly. Using her talons to dig into the fleshy part of his body, she carried him high into the sky, then flung him into the air, only to catch him in flight between her jaws, careful not to kill him—yet. The taste of his blood was bitter and made her feel a bit sick. But his screams were satisfying enough.

She flew higher and higher, then released the man, letting him fall to a horrifying death, only to land next to him and set him aflame. And still the pain she felt was hot and burning in her belly. She unleashed her fire into the sky with fury as her brood appeared in countless numbers, swarming in through the gateways throughout the realm.

Areve tried desperately to return to the dark void, where there was no pain, no anger, and no memory. Where there was only silence. But the flicker in her heart that she didn't even want to try to understand would not allow her to go back. Annoyed and bitter, she circled her tight quarters and began listening to the whispers of her family. *There are so few of them,* she thought. It was hard to distinguish between those who were still close and the haunting voices of the many lost souls, so she closed her eyes and, for the moment, let the sadness of broken pride and defeat fill her. Then, for the good of the realm and those few who were left, she went to the place inside herself where hope still thrived and began the process of forgiveness.

***

Sabastian flew alongside Tobias. He was apparently in no hurry to return to the compound, letting the horse lead him, lost in his own thoughts. Sabastian did not try to hear them. He felt Tobias needed to work out his own private thoughts. *Sad boy, happy boy. Feeling sadness, then joy, then sadness again. Nope, not an easy task, too hard, too tiring. Can't do it, can't help. Just fly, just fly. Stay close.* Sabastian's eyes moved in all directions. *Watch for birds!* He sighed again. *No birds. No leafy trees. No more birds.*

Sabastian's mind wandered, replaying how he could have possibly stopped all this madness, all this sorrow. *We tried so hard. We tried to tell them. But no one heard. No one heard. Couldn't hear.* He slowed his flight so as not to get too far ahead of Tobias. And then the sadness came as his own memories of the beginning circled in his mind. *Heather could hear, Tobias could hear. But no one listened. The General was so full of fear, so many kinds of fear. No understanding. No listening. Only fear and pride inside him. I tried to listen to his thoughts. But could not, could not. Too much sludge in his mind and around his heart, too much. I told Rem I could not hear the General, told him the reasons. But Rem could hear Heather and would not give up. She was not used to the language, but her thoughts were of negotiation, peace, and frustration. How could she make Cornelius understand? How could she assist when Cornelius had so much pride and would not listen? "I am here to contain them. I am here to train them. I am the one they chose to make all the realms safe," he would argue. "They don't understand anyway, they are beasts!" Nope, he could not hear. Heather never stopped trying to make him listen. Not even after her death. Sad, so sad.*

Sabastian noticed he had flown too far ahead of Tobias and rested on a stump. *It was a bright day when she and Tobias went for a stroll and had a meal in the yard. A bright day when Rem decided to approach her, the day Rem tried to talk to her. He wanted to understand what they were doing there. A bright day that turned dark.* Sabastian felt the guilt and frustration that lingered in his heart. *I was there, I was. I tried to assist. I did, I did. But the bolt that took*

Rem's life flew. I didn't hear his thoughts, I couldn't hear the General's thoughts. I would have warned. I would have. I could only watch as sweet Heather and Tobias stood in shock, as the fire in Rem's eyes dimmed and flickered out. As the flowers and grass withered and browned around his body. And I could only watch as Areve revolted and the battle began. I could only watch as the dragons came in scores through all the gateways, and the Time Keepers closed the gateways when all had arrived so none could leave and do harm to the other realms in their fury. I could only watch as soldiers snatched up Heather and Tobias as she screamed and fought and the boy cried. Too much pain, too much anger. I flew, I flew. I gathered all. We must assist to preserve the lives of our kin. We must.

He put his tiny legs on the side of his head and tried to physically shake the memory out. He relived the sorrow of the day, and the days that followed, while he waited for Tobias to catch up. *I must not abandon him now. There is hope again. There is.*

Then he heard her, a soft whisper. It had been so long. His head popped up and excitement filled him. His whole body began to vibrate, and he flew back to Tobias, circling and weaving around his head. "She is awake! Awake! She is, she is! She is awake. Go to her, Tobias. Go!"

***

When Valeen and Luke returned to their rooms, Val was assaulted with the scent of freshly brewed coffee and warm pastries. As she eagerly pushed open the door, she saw Ian and Laura sitting at the small table. Laura waved them over, half a donut in one hand and a steaming mug of coffee in the other.

"Eez are abulous," she told Val and Luke around a mouthful of donut, gesturing toward the plate of pastries. "Eer's offee oo."

Val couldn't help but chuckle at the sight. "Thanks, I think I'll just have the coffee."

Laura swallowed the donut and sipped her coffee. "What's wrong? What happened?"

Ian looked up from the book he was reading. It was one that had been left on the shelves in their rooms. He waited patiently for Valeen and Luke's response to Laura's question.

"What makes you think something happened?" Val answered, a little annoyed that it took a matter of seconds for Laura to read her.

"Really, Val?"

Valeen exhaled deeply as she sat down at the table and poured a cup of coffee. "Okay, fine," she began, and told them what had happened.

Ian thought about the twinge he'd felt in his belly while they were gone but dismissed it as a reaction to the book he was reading and just sat silent as he listened.

"Do you think you can hear them?" Laura asked. "Do you think they can hear you? Is it like some kind of dog hearing? You know, like one of those whistles?"

It was Luke's turn to laugh. "I don't think it was quite like that. I think it was more like what it was with Mary."

"But still different," Valeen said, remembering what it was like to hear Mary's thoughts when she was trapped in the void of the gateways. "There was a different energy to it . . . something ancient."

Ian glanced down at the book laid out on the table. "These creatures seem to be pretty hostile. Are you sure we're safe to keep looking into this?"

Luke cringed at the word "creature" but understood the reference. There were not many who knew that these beings had souls or could even begin to understand how he felt in their presence. He looked down at the page Ian had open. It was a scene of a dragon with a small child in its jaws, standing over a woman who had obviously been disemboweled.

"That is quite disturbing. But I believe it's inaccurate," he said with disgust and took a swallow of coffee, mostly to wash down the bitterness he tasted in his mouth.

Valeen also looked at what Ian was reading. "I think Mr. Haft, or General or whatever he's calling himself, purposefully left these books in here to try to scare us."

Laura picked up another pastry and leaned over to see what they were all talking about. "Ew," she said, tossing the pastry back onto the plate. "Or to keep us from eating."

Val set her coffee mug on the table and contemplated what she'd felt earlier. "I don't believe those pictures are accurate either. What I heard-slash-felt wasn't hostile. It was more intelligent, civilized, but filled with sorrow, and an almost overwhelming grief." She looked around at the faces staring at her. "I know. It doesn't make sense to me either."

Ian closed the book. "Well, I guess we should go find out what's what. If the only terrible thing is that we get eaten by a dragon, well, who could say they ever had that adventure?" When they all looked at him in astonishment, he continued to try to lighten up the mood. "Well, none of these people in this book are saying it."

Laura scowled. "You're twisted. You know that, right?"

"I just don't believe these books are true either. It's deductive reasoning, you know? Really, how long has Cornelius been here? If these 'beings' are hostile and dangerous, why wouldn't they have eaten someone who so obviously deserved it a long time ago? And why haven't we been set upon? I think they're being held captive for . . . whatever reason. And I think we have a responsibility to help them."

The gravity and passion with which Ian expressed his feelings was a surprise to all of them, even Laura. They all knew that he had a way with animals—knowing what they needed and how they needed it, giving always with honor and respect. It was one of his gifts. But none of them had ever witnessed this kind of outburst. It was kind of refreshing to all of them.

Luke realized he'd misinterpreted Ian's comment earlier about being "safe." It was just Ian's form of sarcasm. "Okay then, let's go find someone with a key to those blasted locks."

***

Tobias strolled into the compound, leading the horse by a single rope. He was prepared with an excuse if anyone asked where he had been. But as he approached the desolate area, there was no one around. The place looked deserted. Relieved, he took the horse to the stables.

He glanced across the yard to where Cornelius kept Areve far from the other buildings. *She's awake. You must go to her.* Sabastian's words circled in his mind. *What I am supposed to do? What's happening? Our guests, did they bring something with them?*

He stroked the horse's neck. "Well, old girl, you have carried enough for one morning," he cooed as put her in her stall and covered her with a blanket. He gathered the gear to put on a young stud that could easily pull the heavy cart he would load meat and fresh straw onto and make his rounds. As he started the mindless tasks he was so used to, his thoughts went to Areve.

As his gift of the dragon language became stronger, he had tried to speak with her first. She was their queen. But when he tried, there was nothing there, only emptiness in her thoughts; she had gone to a dark place. Tobias feared that she would perish, concerned that if she did die, the weak connection that was the life force of all the dragons would be severed. And all of them would be gone. He didn't completely understand how it all worked, but he knew that, in some magical way, they held each other together, sustained the very life force in each other. They used some kind of universal language that only they knew and few could understand. And he was one of the few.

He had read many of the books that had been written about these beings. All were inaccurate. So he kept his own journals, hidden within the walls of his room. Cornelius had no interest in knowing the truth. And Tobias didn't believe it would matter anyway. Cornelius believed the dragons were responsible for the death of his mother and had sent out messages by ravens to those who had sent him here, informing them of what had transpired and what he would need to do. The responses to Cornelius had been filled with commendation and praise. The letters only fueled his beliefs and ego, validating his fears and anger, when the initial act of violence had been his decision alone. It was a resentment that ran deep into Tobias's soul.

He loaded the last of the clean straw and raw meat, climbed up on the cart, and headed down the path to make his rounds. It wasn't really a job to him. He enjoyed spending time with the dragons. He would start with the hatchlings.

From behind the cart, he heard his name being called. When he turned, he saw all four of their guests waving at him.

As Val and the others approached Tobias, Ian felt a tingle run down his spine. *This young man is a kindred spirit,* he thought.

"Good morning, Tobias," Valeen said cheerily.

Tobias's shock at being approached so abruptly kept him from speaking. He only nodded in response.

Val hurried on in spite of the discomfort she felt coming off the young man. "I—we were wondering if you would be willing to show us around? We were hoping to see this realm, and all the beings that live here," she said cryptically.

Tobias just stared at them, disbelieving, confused, and frightened. His mind reeled. *Do they know there is something off? Do they suspect what we have done here?* His heart filled with shame and guilt. *Can I trust them? She called them beings . . .*

When Tobias didn't respond, Val looked around at the others for support.

"Does he understand?" Laura whispered to Ian.

Ian felt something stir inside of him. It was different but still familiar. It was how he connected to his horses back home. "He understands," he told them, and stepped up. "Tobias, we are here to

46

find out what happened. We mean no harm to the dragons. We want to help."

Tobias felt cautious relief and a little terror of what Cornelius would do if he shared too much information. *My father does not know what I know.* In a spur of defiance, he decided to take the risk. "I was about to feed the hatchlings. You are welcome to join me."

He jumped off the cart and led the horse and cart by the ropes to the building where the hatchlings were kept. Valeen and the others followed in silence.

When Tobias slid open the heavy doors, a rush of warm, dank air washed over them. He led the horse and cart in, detached the cart, and walked the horse back out. As they all stepped inside, he closed the door behind them.

"We have to keep them warm," he told them absently.

As her eyes adjusted to the dim lighting, Val noticed large barrels of lighted oil set along the walls about every ten feet. The flames danced in the movement of the air that was let in when they opened the door, and then settled and burned high to illuminate the open space. It looked like a warehouse with short corrals lined up on each side and troughs down the middle aisle. She heard soft growls and sharp chirping sounds coming from the corrals, similar to puppy barks, and a childlike excitement filled her.

"Shush now, I brought visitors," Tobias spoke into the room, then turned back to Val and the others with a half-smile on his face. "They're excited . . . and hungry."

When Tobias started to unload the hay and meat from the cart, Val and Luke stepped up to the first corral and peered in. Ian and Laura went to the other side, doing the same.

Tobias started to stack the hay and meat in front of the corrals; it had become so automatic and routine for him, he just slipped into that easy confidence he always had when he was around these magnificent beings and completely forgot he had other people with him—until Valeen's elated reaction echoed through the open space, making him jump.

"They are adorable!" she said. "Can we go in?"

Tobias's heart warmed at her response. He knew they were not adorable. Hatchlings resembled some kind of mix between a mutated chicken and a hairless cat.

"They would like that," he told them.

Valeen opened the gate and stepped in. There were only two of them.

They immediately began to jump on her legs, making those strange grunts and chirps. She bent down to get a closer look and feel, and was pleasantly surprised; they had tufts of feathers and scales. The feathers felt like the down of chicks, and the scales were soft and flexible. As her eyes adjusted to the light, she could just make out the colors of them shimmering in the firelight. They were opaque, changing and blending as their small bodies wiggled, as if still deciding what color they would be. They bounced off her chest with stubby little legs and nudged her with their snouts. She was in sheer delight.

She looked over and saw Laura sitting on the floor cuddling one that was obviously content curled up in her lap while she gently stroked its back. Ian was standing, holding out a squirming dragon while he inspected its uniqueness. Val laughed out loud at his expression of intrigue and confusion.

Tobias went about changing the straw and feeding the other hatchlings. It didn't take him long. It seemed there were only three corrals to tend to, two of which were occupied by Val and Laura. Val heard him cooing and talking to the other hatchlings that were chirping and growling in the corral he was in. His tone was so caring and sincere, it made her heart warm.

Luke just watched with absolute pleasure. This is what he'd wanted for them. This was the experience he had hoped for.

Tobias stepped into the corral with Valeen, pleased and a little relieved that the hatchlings were preoccupied while he changed out their straw and filled their bowls with food and fresh water from the troughs.

"How many are there?" Valeen asked him.

Tobias shrugged and didn't look up as that familiar shame bubbled in his belly. "There are half a dozen hatchlings and three juveniles—two male, one female. The female, Nica, is almost grown."

"Where are the older ones?" Ian asked from across the room.

Still Tobias kept his head down, focusing on his task. "The older ones are kept in a different building."

"And where are their parents?" Luke interrogated further.

Tobias went stiff, walked out of the corral, and headed purposefully to the corral where Laura and Ian were. He could not answer. The atrocity of what the breeding had become, what he had participated in, was dishonorable and disgraceful. The feeling was overwhelming, and rage filled him. He pushed it down and spoke through gritted teeth.

"There is only one stud—Lixten. He is the son of Rem; he was the elder of this realm. There are . . . were two other females . . . and Areve, Rem's mate. She is now the eldest. The two juvenile males are not used to breed; they're still too young." He wasn't ready to tell them about Praxton just yet.

When there was no reply from any of them, only shocked and disappointed expressions, Tobias continued. He might as well; there was no going back now.

"The eggs are taken from their mothers as soon as they are released, and brought here." He stood and stared down at his feet, waiting for the angry, bitter accusations to fly. He was prepared for the sting of words to pierce his body like sharp daggers. He deserved it.

"Where are the rest of them?" Luke asked. He felt sick and angry. *What a waste. How could anyone do such a thing?* It was obvious this boy was just as sick and disturbed, but helpless.

Tobias gripped the handle of the rake he was holding but still couldn't look these people in the face. There was too much guilt, too much regret.

"Most were killed in the battle. Some just died from sorrow. And the others . . . well . . . during the severing of the lava canals . . . well, it had never been done before and no one knew what they were doing . . ." Silent tears filled his eyes, but he refused to let them fall. Instead he again just waited for the assault.

"The severing of their what?" Ian asked, obviously offended.

"It's how they breathe fire," Luke answered, not taking his eyes off Tobias.

Ian nodded and stepped up behind Tobias. The movement made Tobias cringe, ready for the blow, but instead Ian gently laid a hand on the boy's shoulder.

"How can we help?"

Tobias looked up abruptly at all the faces staring at him, full of compassion and understanding. But before he could speak, the doors slid open and Cornelius stepped in.

"So, what do we have here?" he boomed with false cheer. There was an edge of warning directed at Tobias that none of them missed. The hatchlings scattered and silently huddled in the corners of their stalls.

Luke stepped in front of Tobias, his stance defending and ready for a fight.

Tobias went tense again but cleared his throat. "Our . . . um, guests . . . wanted to see the dragons. . . . I . . . thought it . . . I thought it would be okay, as the hatchlings are harmless."

Val watched Cornelius's face go red and his chest puff out, and was infuriated as she watched Tobias shrink at the gesture.

"General, please forgive us. We didn't mean to offend you. And might I add, I speak for all of us . . ." She looked around at all of them, with a little extra warning glance at Luke. ". . . when I say it is an honorable thing you did to step up and assist in the care of these beautiful souls when their parents perished from that horrible disease," she finished.

Ian's and Laura's jaws dropped open. Luke just stared at her in disbelief. Cornelius's chest puffed out bigger at the compliment, and his hostility dissipated.

Tobias's wide-eyed, stunned expression would have made Val laugh if the situation hadn't been so dire. He glanced at his father and then back at Val.

"Please excuse me," he said to all of them as he maneuvered out around Luke. "I have chores to finish."

Cornelius didn't step aside as Tobias hurried out but glanced over his shoulder at his son's retreating back. *The boy did not betray me,* he thought in wonderment. *I always thought he would if given the chance.* He turned around to face his guests with a smug grin on his face.

"Well, I will have the cook make up some soup and fresh bread for you. It's going to be another cool day," he announced, as if every day was not a cool, dreary day.

"That would be wonderful, thank you. We'll be right behind you," Valeen said smoothly.

When Cornelius left without closing the doors, everyone just stared at Valeen.

"Wow. How often do you lie like that to me?" Laura asked. "I'm actually quite impressed."

Val peered out the open door to make sure Cornelius was gone. "Never, but it's obvious that boy is terrified of that horrible man. And I think the General is a little off in the head. Who knows what other damage he could do?" She wrapped her arms around her chest, trying to warm the chill in her bones that wasn't entirely from the cool air. "We should get those doors closed."

Luke stepped up to her and put his arm around her waist, kissing her temple. "We should leave these babes to eat and get warm. Let's go get some warm food in us; we'll try to meet up with Tobias later."

Ian helped Laura back to her feet and held the corral gate open for her. "I think he'll be finding us."

Laura walked out of the corral, brushing the dust and straw off the back of her pants. "I hope so. Did you see his reaction to the General? He might be too afraid."

Val bent down into the corral one last time to stroke and ruffle the hatchlings' heads. "We're going to fix this," she told them, and walked out with the others, closing the door behind them.

CHAPTER *Six*

Tobias walked his horse back to get another cart and restocked it. In his confusion and terror, he had left the one he had in with the hatchlings. It didn't matter; he would go retrieve it later. As he made his way toward Lixten's lair, his mind wandered back to the conversation he'd had with Valeen and the others.

"How can we help?" Is that what the man said—Ian, that is his name—? And that fantastic story Valeen told Cornelius, what was that all about? The only disease this place had was Cornelius. Why would she do that? Could they really help?

He made his mind go blank as he approached Lixten's building. Lixten had never spoken to him. He would stay curled in a dark corner and watch him work, but he wasn't sure he wanted Lixten to know what was happening in his mind until he himself had sorted it all out.

Tobias jumped down from the bench of the cart and moved to the back, where he climbed back on and began shoving bales of hay off the side. He jumped down again and pushed the button that would open the heavy steel doors. They were too big to open manually. Lixten's lair was huge. It had to be—and still it was tight and confined for the size of him.

Thick chains clanked as the doors slowly slid open and he stepped in. *Your Majesty,* he thought, and bowed into the darkness. There was no response, which wasn't unusual, but still he felt he should be respectful and honor who and what the dragon represented. *I have brought you fresh bedding and food. May I enter?* He asked every time. And every time he felt, rather than heard, Lixten's indifference.

Tobias never felt fear of the dragons. They really did have a peaceful way about them, unless provoked. The problem was nobody understood or tried to understand. Sabastian had told him that the dragonflies would go out to the other realms before the dragons came, announcing their arrival. None of them had ever thought that no one could understand what they were saying, so they'd assumed livestock had been left out as offerings to them. They never ate or attacked humans—they didn't care for the taste, for one thing, and actually had respect for other beings. Dragons were great observers. They watched what the beings in other realms ate and how they attained it, and just did the same. *Well, not exactly the same,* Tobias thought, recalling Praxton's eating habits.

"There are guests in the realm?" a deep, rumbling voice said from one of the dark corners of the building.

Tobias froze, stunned and shocked. None of the dragons ever *spoke* out loud to him. He didn't even know that they knew the language—except Praxton, but Tobias was the one who'd taught him.

A small flutter of wings in the barred light from the ceiling caught his attention. Without thinking, he moved outside, hit the button to close the doors, and quickly ducked back in. He ran to one of the barrels of oil and dug a match out of his pocket. Fumbling with excitement, he dropped it on the ground twice before he managed to light the barrel, then ran and lit two more.

Lixten was still in the shadows. Tobias heard the rattle of the chains that bound Lixten's legs, and the sound made him sick. Lixten was magnificent. Tobias vaguely remembered seeing him in flight when he was young; the impression had stuck with him all these years. He tried not to remember, seeing what had become of this majestic being: His once-vibrant orange and blue colors were now faded, and his wings had been cut unceremoniously and the edges left jagged. The skin between the bones was thinning and had an ashy color. His wings had not been fully extended since he was confined to this building. He stood two floors high and thirty feet wide. The sheer volume of his presence could scare the hells out of anyone. Even Cornelius didn't venture in here very often.

When Lixten finally moved into the light, Tobias knelt and bowed his head. *Your Majesty.*

Lixten moved like lightning. His head swung down within a few feet of Tobias's face and stopped abruptly. "Do not call me that."

"I . . . I apologize, Your Maj—I apologize."

Lixten did not reply and slowly moved back. Tobias just stood silent in complete awe. He had never interacted with Lixten before and was not completely sure what to do. For the first time in a long time, he had the chance to really look at him in the light. Lixten had scars from the wounds he'd sustained in the battle along his sides and shoulders. Even his leg had a small gouge just above the knee. And then there was the one very prominent scar along the side of his neck where they had severed his lava canal. It was done without precision or care. Tobias looked away, ashamed. *How could I have let this happen?*

"You did not," Lixten said with authority, reading his thoughts. Then he sighed and spoke softly. "I did."

"Did not, did not. Neither, did not!" Sabastian chattered as he swooped down from the opening in the bars.

Tobias startled. "Sabastian, what are you doing here? You know it is dangerous for you to be this close."

"I am stealthy, I am safe. I fly like the wind." To prove his point, he buzzed by Tobias's ears.

"So you keep saying," Tobias retorted, and swatted at Sabastian as he passed in front of his face. "Stop that!" he scolded the dragonfly, his distraction only momentary.

Lixten stood, lifting his head within inches of the barred ceiling, peering out the bars longingly. "Stop your rambling, Sabastian, or I will eat you myself," he grumbled, not looking away from his limited view of the outside.

The awe returned in Tobias as he heard the idle threat. "You can speak?"

"Yes, yes, he can," Sabastian prattled.

Lixten again moved quick as a snake, swinging his head and snapping at Sabastian. But Sabastian was quicker and zipped out of the way, flying up to land on one of the bars in the ceiling. Lixten sighed again. "Yes, I can speak the language of man."

"But why . . . ? How . . . ?" Tobias stammered. He composed himself as the anger filled him. "Why didn't you tell anyone? Why did you not try to speak to Cornelius when he first arrived here? All of this . . ." Tobias opened his arms to encompass the room. "All of this could have been avoided! All the death could have been stopped." He was on the verge of hysterics, not sure where it came from—and then, realizing he was yelling at a dragon, he stopped abruptly.

Lixten was not affected. He just sank to the floor heavily, causing the whole building to shudder under his weight. "I did not know it fluently. I was still young and learning. And my own arrogance did not allow for me to care enough to learn the tongue of man. And then Rem was slain, and I only felt rage and revenge in my heart."

"Yes, young, and arrogant, yes. But I teach him. I did, I did. I tell stories. Too stubborn, yep," Sabastian chattered from the safety of the ceiling bar.

Lixten just glared up at him, and then let out a heavy breath. "Yes, I learned, but it was too late. I had already surrendered. I needed to save what lives I could. It was my duty." The tone of Lixten's words did not reflect nobility. They were full of shame and regret. Tobias knew the feeling well.

The exhaustion from the day's events was starting to catch up with him. He sat heavily on the cold concrete floor, his mind beginning to reel. *What did they say? They could help? How? It could be dangerous. Show them the journals. How do I keep Cornelius from finding out? What about Praxton . . . ?*

Who is Praxton? Lixten's voice echoed in his thoughts.

"What?" Tobias shook his head. "What?"

I can still hear you. You have your mother's gift. But you have mastered the Quiet Place. Just not right now, Lixten thought to him with humor.

"The what place?" Tobias asked.

"The Quiet Place. Every being in all the worlds is entitled to the Quiet Place. It's the place where you can go to be completely alone, without being disturbed," Lixten told him.

"Yes, yes. The Quiet Place," Sabastian repeated somberly. "Don't get stuck, nope, nope. Areve was stuck, yes, yes, it is sad." He fluttered down from the bars and landed on Lixten's snout, gripping one nostril with his tiny legs, looking him directly in the eyes. "But now she is awake! Awake. My Majesty, she's awake. Tobias can talk to her. He has already told some of his secrets. He has, he has," he said excitedly.

Tobias stood quickly. "Sabastian, you don't know what you're talking about, be quiet!"

Lixten huffed air out his nose, causing Sabastian to tumble backwards in the air. "He's right, Sabastian. You talk nonsense. I have imprisoned what is left of my tribe; there is no hope. Leave me now. I wish to be alone . . ."

Tobias felt Lixten go deep inside—to 'the Quiet Place,' he guessed—and knew they were done talking for today. He felt a bit of relief and a bit of disappointment. There was so much to sort through, but maybe there was still hope.

He looked around and realized he had locked himself in. The only way to open the door was from the outside. He spotted the pipe that was used to fill the trough of water and followed its path to the opening in the roof. "Well, I guess that will work."

He started to climb, using the brackets as handholds and moving slowly, as the metal was slick with condensation from the heat coming off the barrels of lit oil. He glanced up to gauge his distance. *Only a few more feet . . .* His foot slipped and he lost his grip. He felt himself falling and closed his eyes, waiting for the impact of the concrete floor.

But his bones didn't rattle and snap. Instead he heard his body slap against flesh, and then he was soaring up and up.

When he opened his eyes, he was staring into the bulging eyes of Sabastian. The small insect reached out a tiny, sticky leg and touched his face. "You are safe, you are."

Behind Sabastian he saw two very large gray eyes staring back at him. He had landed on Lixten. He felt a little terrified. *What if Lixten thought it was some kind of attack?*

Don't be ridiculous, boy, he heard Lixten growl in his thoughts, obviously insulted. *You were falling.*

Lixten lifted him to the barred ceiling. Tobias's stomach tickled, and an unfamiliar pleasure washed over him. He couldn't stop the giggle that escaped his throat. In that moment, he imagined what it would be like to ride on the back of Lixten, soaring through the open skies.

When he reached the top, he climbed through the bars and out onto the roof. He knelt down on all fours and peered through the bars, excitement still vibrating through him, but Lixten was already turning away, disappearing into the shadows. Disappointment immediately replaced his delight. "Thank you, Lixten," he mumbled as he crawled to the edge of the building and began to shimmy down the steel rails.

He let himself fall the last few feet, went to the front of the building, and pushed the button to open the doors. Lixten was in the shadows and silent. Even Sabastian was silent, so Tobias went about finishing his tasks, raking out and replacing the straw and dumping the mounds of raw meat into an empty trough. He looked around to check his work and saw that the barrels of oil were still aflame.

"I'll leave these burning; the night will be chilly." When there was no response, he turned and left. Pushing the button again, he stood and stared into the gloom of Lixten's lair until the doors closed in front of him. A new kind of sorrow engulfed him. *We have to fix this,* he thought, and looked up to the house. *Can I trust them?*

With a deep sigh, he turned away to finish his chores. He was already behind schedule, but the events of the day circled in his mind, desperately searching for a solution.

When Lixten heard the doors clang shut, he opened his eyes. His loneliness wriggled like snakes in his belly as he stared longingly at the flames in the barrel. It had been a long time since he'd allowed himself to wish for his fire.

***

Tobias's last stop was Areve's lair. *She's awake.* Sabastian's words echoed in his mind. He stood outside the steel doors, the cart and horse behind him, staring. Her lair was as big as Lixten's, as she wasn't much smaller than him. He was unsure of what he could say to her, if she talked to him at all. Maybe Sabastian was wrong.

Come inside, Tobias. I wish to speak with you, he heard Areve's voice say in his mind. At least, he thought it was hers. He had never heard what she sounded like before. It wasn't hostile or threatening, but it was commanding.

He reached out and hit the button and stood still while the doors clanged open completely. He managed to get a hold of himself and quickly stepped inside and knelt to one knee. *Your Majesty.*

"You may stand. I am old; I am not your queen," he heard a soft, regal voice say.

It surprised Tobias that suddenly the dragons had become so chatty. *What is happening?* he thought.

"I was hoping you could tell me, young Tobias."

Tobias lifted his head and stood slowly, not sure his legs would hold him up. "I'm . . . I'm not sure what you mean, Your Maj—ma'am." He realized they were speaking out loud and jerked around to peer out the open doors.

If it makes you worry so, we can speak in the language of my tribe, Areve told him.

It did make him nervous, but he wasn't quite as willing to lock himself in a dragon's lair again. So he pulled out his matches and lit the barrels along the walls of Areve's lair to keep her warm.

You are a kind boy, Tobias. Thank you. Can you tell me what brought me from the Quiet Place?

Tobias went out to the cart and began unloading the meat and straw for Areve, searching the grounds for anyone who might be out in the rain and hear their conversation. Unloading the cart was an automatic task, so he was able to still carry on a conversation without anyone noticing.

I do not—I don't know what is happening, or why. It might be our guests. I think they brought magic with them. I . . . I think they might be able to help.

Areve stepped into the light from the barrels. *Guests? Tell me about them.*

Again Tobias's breath was taken away by the vision of these beings. She was big, yes. But also sleek and refined. Her presence was of regal beauty and stance. Her colors were soft pink, lavender, and indigo; although faded, they blended silkily down her body to the tip of her tail.

Tobias grunted, lifting a bale of hay from the cart. "I don't really know that much about them. They've only been here a couple of days, and I have only talked to them once, in the hatchery." He cringed at the memory of Cornelius coming in and interrupting them.

Areve came further out into the light. *There are hatchlings? How many?*

There was a hint of excitement in the question. But Tobias's heart broke. He dumped a large pail of raw meat into a trough, wiped his forehead with his arm, and stared at his feet. How could he answer?

I know there are some still alive. I can hear them. But I can't hear the hatchlings; they're too young. Tobias, how many? That commanding voice again.

Tobias dropped his shoulders and looked up to the barred ceiling. "There are six, Majesty."

For what seemed like a lifetime, there was no response at all from Areve, and Tobias felt that any further communication was lost.

I see, he finally heard her say. A deep sadness echoed through him. He wasn't sure if it was his sadness or hers. More than likely it was both.

He slowly turned around to face her. "I am sorry. I have tried to save as many as I could. I just didn't know how."

Something inside him broke open, and he fell to his knees. Not from fear that Areve would cause him harm, but from a trust and love he hadn't felt since his mother died. Something took hold of his emotions; it felt out of his control, and he could not stop the flow as he surrendered to it and sobbed.

"I am afraid all the time. Afraid of what Cornelius would do, afraid of what I can hear, and what I can feel from you and the other dragons. Afraid of causing more harm than good, afraid that Cornelius will send me away, afraid that I will let him down . . ." His last statement caught him by surprise. *Is that true?*

He startled when he felt something cool and soft rub the top of his head and his cheek. Areve had bent down to comfort him with her snout. He felt her understanding and compassion, and he felt her sorrow. He wrapped his arms around her neck, and together they cried and mourned until both were drained.

When Tobias stood and wiped his face, then Areve's, with his sleeve, he felt a little lighter. He looked Areve in the eyes. "We can fix this. I don't know how yet. But I think we have been sent help from the higher realms."

And what of Praxton? Areve asked him.

Tobias was taken aback. He had tried so hard to keep Praxton from his conscious thoughts. It felt too dangerous to even let the dragons know of his existence. "You saw that, huh?"

Areve smiled. *Yes, I saw that.*

"I don't know what I was thinking. I just wanted to do something, anything. It was a risky, stupid thing." Tobias started to pace, throwing his arms in the air. "I don't even know where he is. I've been to his cave twice now, and he has been nowhere in sight. I know he's a dragon and has more survival instinct than I'll ever know. But he's young still and untrained and—"

He abruptly stopped pacing and looked up at Areve's scowling face. "I can't believe I just said that. He doesn't need training." He threw his head back and shut his eyes, letting a groan escape his throat. "What am I doing?"

I believe Praxton is fine. Talk to your friends. I am hungry and wish to eat and ponder my own thoughts now.

"Oh. Of course. I apologize." Tobias hastily gathered his buckets, rake, and shovels. "I will leave. I think I still have time to go check on Praxton, get him something to eat." He stopped with his arms full but still managed a bow. "Thank you," he told her, and turned to leave.

Tobias.

Yes, ma'am? he answered, turning to face her.

You are doing just fine. You have done a good thing with Praxton.

Tobias nodded and smiled. *Yes, ma'am.*

And Tobias.

He turned to face her again. *Yes, ma'am?*

Please call me Areve.

His smile widened, and his chest filled with joy and pride. It was an honorable gift to be allowed to be so informal with the royal family. He nodded again. *Yes, Your Ma—Areve.*

CHAPTER *Seven*

There was an icy rain all the next day, so Valeen and the others stayed inside, only seeing glimpses of Tobias through the windows as he ran from building to building. Valeen had considered going out in search of the young man but decided it would be a waste of time. She would just end up playing a game of hide-and-seek that Tobias wouldn't know he was playing.

Cornelius had become a ghost to his guests, but Pip had been a constant interruption, coming in with food and checking the fires, cleaning up, or doing other menial tasks. He had come in several times just to see if they needed anything, and Valeen began to get suspicious. Every time they started a conversation about the possibilities of freeing this realm, there was Pip with some nonsense announcement. It was obvious he'd been instructed to not let them be alone for too long.

Pip had managed to find a pad of paper and pencils at Ian's request. And venturing outside was not an option due to the bone-chilling rain, so instead they stayed in by the fires and chatted idly. While they talked about nothing, Ian sketched. His vivid recollection of the hatchlings was impressive.

"Wow, those are great," Laura told him, leaning over his shoulder. "Too bad you don't have color."

"I do at home. I can finish them there." Ian studied his work for a moment, then tossed the pad on the table. "We should find the rest of them."

"We should," Luke agreed, sitting up in the chair and resting his elbows on his knees. "We know where they are kept. But there is a reason they have not fought back. Something happened, and that's what we have to find out first."

Val moved to sit on the arm of Luke's chair. "By my calculations, there are only about twelve or thirteen left. What happened to the rest of them? Cornelius couldn't have killed them all, could he?"

No one answered. They just looked at each other; none of them wanted to think about what could have happened to the rest, let alone speak it out loud.

Laura glanced out the window. "I think it's getting dark. We can go search for Tobias first thing in the morning." She went to close the door to their rooms and locked it just to be safe, not realizing that Pip had not left the hallway.

"We should come up with a plan. There is more to this realm than just this compound," Luke told them.

"Maybe we can set up some kind of excursion tour. You know, like on horseback or something?" Ian added.

Val stood and went to the window. The icy drizzle was dissipating, but the dismal gloom remained. "That seems like a start. Maybe our friendly concierge Pip can assist us."

***

Pip was crouched behind one of the statues, doing his best to listen, but only getting bits and pieces of the conversation. When they closed the door, he only heard muffled voices. Deflated, he wiggled out from behind the statue and hurried down the stairs.

Were they talking about the dragons? Do they want to save them? That is crazy! Do they not realize the beasts are dangerous? And what was that about Tobias? Should I tell the General? What would I tell him? I couldn't hear anything clearly. I am not sure what they were talking about, and that could upset him. I don't want to disturb the General with something I don't know for sure. Besides, he's been locked in his rooms for the last couple of days, obviously not wanting to be bothered.

Pip had not seen the General except out in the yard. He had not approached Pip at all. He would go out and walk the grounds and then come back and go straight to his rooms again. It wasn't unusual for the General not to talk to him. He spent most of his time alone anyway. But the General had given him a job to do. *I guess I've been doing it. The General only told me to keep a watch on them and prevent them from going into forbidden areas.*

Pip stopped in front of his quarters, fishing the key out of his pocket. *What exactly are the forbidden areas?* he wondered again. He hadn't questioned the first time Cornelius mentioned these mysterious places. When the General gave him his assignment, he was eager to do it. He was so eager to please the man he would have agreed to anything, even if he didn't understand what exactly it was.

He shrugged a shoulder and stepped through the door, softly closing and locking it behind him. "I'll do better tomorrow," he said to the empty room.

***

Tobias left Areve's lair and headed into the forest. He wanted to tell Praxton of his meeting with Areve. But there was no sign of him. While he waited, he shivered in the rain, pulling the collar of his light jacket up around his neck and blowing warmth into his hands. His mind wandered, going through every horrible scenario that could have happened, until he was too wet and cold to stay any longer. Shadows of darkness had started to creep through the trees, and he had to get back. So he left the meat he brought and headed for the house.

Not even Sabastian had made an appearance. Disturbed, Tobias had kept searching the trees and skies for any sign of Praxton while Rosy sauntered through the trees. *Where could he have gone? Why would he leave?* Sorrow from the possible loss filled his heart. *Could Cornelius have found him? Is he now waiting with Praxton strung up and gutted until I return? So he can gloat?* The very idea and vision made Tobias sick, and he fought to stay atop Rosy and not retch.

It was dark when Tobias entered his rooms. A mixture of annoyance and terror swarmed in his belly. He had made it back, and to his relief, the house and grounds were quiet and deserted. He now sat on his bed. Worry and hope circled in his mind, and as if the thoughts themselves were starting to crowd inside his head, it became heavy and began to droop until his chin rested on his chest.

Get a hold of yourself, Tobias! Praxton is probably off exploring somewhere. Or found a bigger place to get out of the rain. He knows the danger.

He thumbed through his journals but could not bring himself to put into writing his notions of Praxton's disappearance. Instead his mind wandered to the day Lixten surrendered, remembering the horror of what he'd witnessed and the strange, agonizing discomfort he felt while watching from the balcony of his mother's now-empty rooms, where only the lingering of her perfume and the distance of her soul remained.

Lixten had been staked to the ground, chains wrapped around his snout. Blood trickled from the wounds, blackening the ground where it dripped. Tobias remembered the look in Lixten's eyes as he glanced up at him, making eye contact. He heard his mother's voice in his head. *Move away, Tobias. Go find Pip.* He had wished desperately for her to wrap him in her arms so he could cry on her shoulder, but the General had come in, and he would not have his son bellowing like a girl. Tobias had swallowed his sorrow and stuffed the pain deep inside, burying it with indifference, and walked back into his mother's rooms and didn't leave. Eventually Pip had found him, and together they had witnessed the horrific events unfold.

Tobias sighed and shook the memory away, trying to focus on his journals. Not knowing what to do next, he decided to not think about any of it anymore. He was just too tired. Even though he was restless with concern about Praxton, he was still unsure if he could trust Valeen and the others, and uncertain of what Cornelius would do or even what he might be capable of. *Could he really cause harm to another human being?*

Exhaustion got the better of him, and he began drifting off to sleep, the screams of men and dragons echoing in his mind.

***

Cornelius sat in a wide high-backed chair, staring out the barred window of his private rooms. But he wasn't seeing the gray, gloomy skies, the barren ground, or the dry, skeletal trees. He was replaying that dreadful day, the day his heart turned to stone and his soul went small and hid deep within him, unable to admit his decisions might have been irrational. The terror he felt when the dragon king landed beside his wife and young son still bubbled in his heart.

Did the dragon king really mean to harm them? Could there have been any truth in Heather's words? Was it not just the whimsical thoughts and feelings of a woman? Could there have been a way to communicate with them?

As the questions circled, his mind moved back to the memory of that day. *She was so angry.* He had never seen her so enraged, or so heartbroken. They were arguing. *Heather was hysterical, and I was angry . . .*

Cornelius closed his eyes and tried to push the memory away, but it came anyway. *They were on the balcony; Heather had wanted to take the argument away from Tobias. He was already in a state of shock and terror.* Cornelius remembered the silent tears that ran steady from his son's eyes and the distant stare as he stood still, with young Pip doing his best to comfort him. Burying the emotion he felt for his son, he had followed Heather out. *She was screaming and crying, her words making no sense. She was accusing him of using her and their son as bait, with no regard for their safety.* He had just wanted her to calm down, be rational. He wanted to pull her close, explain how an irrational terror overtook him when he saw Rem land so close to her and Tobias. He was trying to protect them.

But when I reached for her, she yanked away from me and stumbled backwards, tumbling over the railing. I saw the sudden clarity of shock on her face as I tried to grab her, the feeling of her fingers slipping through mine. The grief was too much for him to bear, and the only thing he could feel was rage. *They were wild, mindless, murdering beasts, and it was my job to contain them, keep them from the other realms as I alone saw fit. It was my duty. I had no choice.*

He knew what they all thought. No one asked what happened; they only saw Heather fall and him leaning over the railing, looking down at the lifeless body of the woman he supposedly loved more than anything. His thoughts had been racing, trying to make sense of what he had just witnessed. He had turned around to see the shocked and terrified expression of Pip and the still-distant but devastated stare of his son. He tried to speak, but no words would come, so he dismissed it and ran past them, leaving them alone as he made his way down to where Heather's body was lying.

He vividly remembered the silence in the air; it was like all the life in the realm had been sucked out. Then there was a sudden burst of chaos as men began running and the dragons began circling with weapons and fire. Blood and screams erupted around him as he knelt next to the broken body of his beloved.

And something inside him broke. The force of the steel walls that slammed shut around his mind and heart sent him into the state of an emotionless mission of defense. He left Heather's body where it was, engaging in the battle without another thought or feeling. He began shouting orders and directing his men into combat. Those beasts had just murdered his wife. As irrational as the thought was, it had become his truth. All that was left in his soul was a sense of duty.

He remembered the look on Tobias's face, the shock and the disbelief, and the hate. Pip was but a toddler, but Tobias was old enough to remember what he saw. *He knew it was an accident, right? He saw his mother lose her balance and fall. It was an accident. An accident that was caused by the dragons. They did this. They killed my sweet Heather and forced me to take action. I did what I had to, for the safety of my men and all the realms.*

***

Ian got up early, making his way to the kitchen. As he'd suspected, it was on the main floor, toward the back of the house. It was a large open space, except for the long wooden table down the center of the room with stools tucked neatly underneath. *Enough room to prepare meals for an army,* he thought. The counters were stainless steel that encased a large oven, a freezer, and a double-door refrigerator. There were three doors to what he assumed was a pantry and closet and probably an access to servant quarters. There was a darkened entryway with stairs leading up, which he assumed again was a back entrance to the other rooms in the house. Obviously, its purpose was to provide a more discreet way for the help to travel through the house, he mused.

He spotted the coffee pot on one of the counters and began searching through cupboards and the pantry for the coffee and mugs. One of the doors opened and a sleepy Pip emerged, rubbing his eyes. He froze in his tracks when he spotted Ian, and both just stared at each other. It was obvious Ian would have to make the first move.

"Good morning, Pip," he said casually, and went about the task of making coffee. He moved to the sink and began filling the pot with water, glancing over his shoulder to see if Pip had moved. He hadn't. He stood where he was, wide-eyed and silent.

Ian shut off the water without turning around and filled the water chamber on the coffee pot. "I was just making coffee. Would you like some?"

When there was no response from Pip, he tried a different approach. "Does the General make you sleep in that closet?"

Pip's thoughts raced in his head, the grogginess fighting its way to clarity. At first he was startled, which made the adrenaline ignite in his body while his mind fought to catch up. *Why is there a strange man in the house? No, not a stranger—one of the guests. Ian? What is he saying? Coffee? I don't drink coffee. Does the General make me sleep in the closet?*

"What? No! Of course not," he heard himself say out loud, the sound of his own voice making him jump a little. He turned around to see where he'd come from and thought it did look like a door to a closet. "It's the passageway to my rooms," he told Ian, a bit more defensively than he intended.

Ian nodded. "Well, are you hungry?"

The question was asked with gentle sincerity, and Pip felt himself physically and mentally relax. "Um, I was . . . I was just going to get me some milk and crackers."

Ian opened the double-door fridge and peered in. "That doesn't sound like a very filling breakfast. There has to be something in here we can make," he continued casually.

Pip stood where he was. "I don't know how to cook, and Ruben has gone through the gateway to get more supplies. He gave me instruction to prepare cold cuts and crackers for your meals until he returns." *Why are you talking to this man? Stop talking, Pip!* He felt a stir in him. *What does it matter? What am I so afraid of? There is something, something about this man that feels safe.* There was that voice again. *You can trust him, Pip.*

Ian watched Pip working out something in his own head and waited, holding a carton of eggs and sliced ham in his hands, to see if there was anything else Pip wanted to add. He used his foot to close the door to the fridge and shrugged his shoulders. "Well, it just so happens I know how to cook. Why don't you come and sit down? I'll teach you." He gestured to one of the stools at the table.

Pip could only stand where he was, unsure of how to respond.

Ian set the eggs and ham on the counter. "Maybe you could help me find the pans to cook in?"

Pip's thoughts finally landed. *There is no harm in a meal.* He shrugged one shoulder and went to one of the lower cupboards, pulled out two frying pans, and put them on the stove. "The coffee mugs are in the cupboard on the other side of the sink," he told Ian as he sat down at the table.

"Thank you," Ian told him, sensing that he was still feeling uneasy. "Are you sure you don't want any coffee?"

Pip lowered his head and grinned, something he hadn't done in a long time. "Yes, sir, I'm sure."

"Okay, a glass of milk it is, then. But you don't know what you're missing. I make a mean cup of coffee," Ian told him lightheartedly.

A giggle bubbled up out of Pip. It felt strange and warm. Something else he hadn't felt in a long time. "No thank you, sir."

As Ian made them breakfast, the conversation was light. They talked about what Pip did there, what chores he had. Pip even felt comfortable and safe enough to tell Ian about his paintings.

"I'd love to see them before we go," Ian told him.

Pip's face lit up at the request; the expression softened his sharp features and made him appear more his age. It occurred to Ian that Pip was no more than two or three years younger than Tobias. He imagined it was a hard, lonely life Pip had here that had made him seem so young and frail.

Before Pip could respond, they both turned to the sound of footsteps coming up from one of the stairways that Ian had assumed was the way to the servants' quarters. Tobias came in with his head down, still tucking one side of his shirt into his pants. Movement out of the corner of his eye made him stop in his tracks the same way Pip had when he first came in, doing a double take at Ian, then making eye contact with Pip, who had gone quiet, studying his eggs. Although the grogginess Ian saw in Pip's eyes was not there, the surprise followed by confusion was the same on Tobias. Ian filed away the interaction between them to ponder another time.

"Good morning, Tobias. Would you like to join us for some ham and eggs?" he asked cheerfully. "I wanted to ask you about something anyway."

Tobias tore his gaze away from Pip. His shock of seeing Pip smiling and talking openly with another human being, let alone a stranger, would have to wait until later. He adjusted the waistband of his pants. "Um . . . sure." He took a plate out of the cupboard. "What do you want to ask me?" he asked, trying to keep his voice casual while his heart pounded in his chest.

Ian sipped his coffee and deliberately set it softly on the table, afraid that any sudden movements would have both these boys running. "Well, we—Laura and I, and Val and Luke—were wondering if maybe we could take a ride today. You know, on horseback to get a look around at our surroundings?"

Tobias was grateful that he had his back facing Ian, but he couldn't stop his body from tensing, causing eggs to spill off the spoon he was using to scoop them from the pan.

Ian didn't miss his reaction, or Pip's: The boy dropped his fork, making a clanking sound when it hit his plate. Ian watched as the boy went visibly pale. He reached across the table, resting his hand on Pip's arm.

"Are you okay, Pip?" he asked, genuinely concerned. "Are you sick? You're more than welcome to join us if you feel up to it."

Ian hadn't thought it was possible, but Pip's horrorstruck face turned even more ghostly white. He dropped his head into his chest. "May I be excused, please?" he mumbled.

"What is it, Pip? Did I say something wrong?" Ian pleaded, not sure what was happening.

Pip didn't look up, didn't speak, just stared at his buttons.

Ian put his hands in the air and let them fall to his knees. "What is going on in this place? What kind of madness—" He stopped abruptly when he noticed Pip's shoulders slump deeper.

"Oh, shit, I'm so sorry, Pip."

Tobias leaned down and whispered in Pip's ear. "You may be excused . . . brother."

Pip's head jerked up, and he just stared at Tobias. Tobias grinned and nodded. Pip grinned back at him and hurried from the table, retreating to his rooms.

Tobias took his place at the table, sliding Pip's plate aside and setting his own down. Ian took a deep breath and waited for Tobias to get settled and explain what just went on. But before Tobias could say anything, Valeen burst through the door.

"I told you I could smell coffee. He's in here," she said, looking over her shoulder to Laura and Luke, who followed behind her.

"And you made breakfast," Laura announced as she leaned over and kissed his cheek sloppily.

Ian put aside the tension he was feeling for now, filed away like the exchange between Tobias and Pip. "How do you know it was me? Tobias here could have made it." He lifted his mug and gestured toward the young man.

"I know it was you, Ian," Valeen replied while filling her cup. "The eggs are scrambled, and the ham is only half warm."

Luke slapped Ian on the shoulder as he made his way to the coffee pot. "Thanks, Ian, I'm starving."

Tobias sat quietly listening to the idle conversation and lighthearted banter. There was something relaxing and soothing in it. *Why do they want to go out in the forest? What are they looking for? What if Cornelius finds out?* His thoughts shifted as panic started to make its way in, oozing through and drowning out the voices around him like hot tar. *What if they run into Praxton? What would Cornelius do if he found out about Praxton? It was the General who brought the eggs to the hatchery—what did he do with the other females?* Tobias quashed the last question as swiftly as it came; he didn't even want to consider what his father did to them. But more questions circled in his mind, and his heart made a decision.

"I'll take you out, if you'd like," he heard himself say out loud. The chatter in the room stopped abruptly.

It was Ian who responded. "Well, all right then. We'll just clean up here and go get some warmer clothes on and then meet you in the stables."

Tobias, still shocked at his own bravery, shrugged a shoulder as he got up to put his plate in the sink. Feeling a little shaky, he sat back down at the table until he felt stable again. "I have a couple of chores that need to be done first. Why don't you meet me in about an hour?"

"Sounds good to me," Laura exclaimed as she jumped up from her stool and headed out of the kitchen. Luke drank the last swallow of coffee, nodded, patted Tobias on the shoulder, then followed Laura out.

Valeen reached across the table and laid her hand on Tobias's arm. Her touch tingled under his skin, and her eyes met his.

"Thank you, Tobias," she told him sincerely, knowing this was probably another direct defiance of Cornelius's rules.

Tobias couldn't take his eyes off her. Her touch and her gentle words stroked the deepest places in him, the places where the memories of his mother lived. *Everything will be all right,* he heard her whisper in his thoughts. Then the spell broke when she released his arm.

"Come on, Ian, let Tobias get his work done," she said cheerfully.

Her words faded into present time, and Tobias had to shake his head to clear the mist. He could only stare at her when she turned from the door and smiled at him before she left.

Ian hastily drank the last of his coffee and began gathering the dishes left on the table. "Thanks for breakfast, Tobias. I couldn't have made it better myself," he joked. When Tobias didn't respond, he just slapped him on the back as he walked by. "I'll have to work on my jokes. We'll see you in a bit."

Tobias was still struggling with his emotions. "Um, okay" was all he could manage to say. He didn't even realize Ian had already left the kitchen.

***

Pip sat on his bed, staring at his drawings he had pinned to the wall, but he wasn't seeing them. His thoughts replayed the morning's events over and over. He liked the man Ian. His kindness seemed genuine, and Pip felt comfortable around him. *He'd like to see my drawings. Nobody's ever asked to see them before. Have I ever told anyone about them?*

'You may be excused, brother.' Tobias called me 'brother.' What

kind of magic did these people bring with them? Was it a trick? They wanted me to go outside. Were they trying to get me to leave, to go through the gateway? There was a time when Tobias would take me out with him. But as he got older he seemed to get sadder, and preferred his own company and the company of the dragons. Pip shuddered at the very idea of being that close to the dragons. His fear had taken complete control over any rational thoughts or feelings, and he'd found himself avoiding Tobias altogether. He would find things to do around the house instead of venturing outside. And it didn't take long for Tobias to quit asking. He would go about his chores and then disappear into the trees for hours, and soon they just drifted apart, each growing into a comfortable aloneness.

"You are excused, brother," Tobias had whispered. The words vibrated through Pip. It had been so long since he felt that kind of joy, even if it was only a flicker in his heart. *What is happening? It has to be some kind of spell. But who would be casting it?* He'd heard the stories when he used to hide in the soldiers' quarters. He heard the dragons had some kind of magic. He heard they could put a man in a trance so they could eat him without him trying to run away.

Pip jumped up and began to pace, chewing on the tip of his thumb. *Is that what is happening? Are the dragons trying to get me to go outside so they can eat me, using Tobias and the others to lure me out? Maybe I should talk to Cornelius about all this. No. He would think I was being silly. He doesn't believe the dragons have any magic. They are wild, dangerous animals and would have killed Heather and Tobias if he hadn't intervened.*

He sat back down on the bed and lowered his head, the sadness seeping into his heart. "They would have killed them, just like they killed my father," he mumbled. Silent tears of loss and confusion ran down his face. Not knowing what to do or who he could trust, he curled up with his pillow and just allowed his sad turmoil to flow.

They feel so safe; maybe I could try to go outside. Do I really want to stay here? There could be more out there in the worlds, a place I wouldn't be so afraid . . .

CHAPTER *Eight*

Tobias finished his chores. He didn't have to feed the dragons today, and he could try to find Praxton later. He began to gather the tack for the horses. Most of the saddles and reins were dusty; he was the only one who used the horses anymore.

Ian sauntered into the stables. "Can I help you with that?" He gestured to the wall where the saddles and bits hung on hooks and stands.

Tobias was a little skeptical. "Do you know how?"

Ian chuckled to himself, thinking about the horse ranch he ran at home. "I know a little about it."

Tobias shrugged. "The saddles should be wiped down. They haven't been used in a while."

Ian nodded and reached for a rag that hung on one of the stable gates, hefted a saddle off one of the stands, and began wiping it down. "Doesn't the General have men to keep up on these things?" he asked casually.

Tobias lifted a clean saddle onto an old mare and began buckling it under her belly. "He sent most of the soldiers home after Lixten surrendered. There were a couple that stayed for a while, but then they just stopped coming back." He never looked away from his task. A rage accompanied with his shame kept him from looking at Ian.

When the saddle was secure, he moved to fit the bit into the mare's mouth and wrap the reins around her neck. "I don't know where they would have gone. Cornelius's selection of soldiers was very specific. I don't think anyone would have called them good men."

Ian nodded again and swung the saddle onto the horse in front him. When the horse fussed and kicked, he ran a gentle hand down his neck, softly cooing, "It's okay, old boy, it's okay." The horse stopped kicking and settled at Ian's soothing touch. When Ian looked over at Tobias, he was staring at him with awe and confusion.

Ian grinned wide. "I have a couple of horses back home. I've done this a time or two."

Tobias lifted another saddle and began cleaning it. "He's not used to being saddled. He was ridden in the battle, and I think he's still a bit skittish, but you seem to have a way with him." He watched Ian saddle the other horses with easy confidence. He shook his head and smiled. "A time or two, huh?"

Ian smiled without looking away from his task. "Yep."

The two of them finished preparing the horses for a day's trip in comfortable silence until the others joined them. When they were all settled and mounted, Tobias led them out and into the bare trees.

There was light conversation between Valeen and the others while they searched the sky and trees for any sign of the amazing beings that once lived here. They tried to keep their thoughts hopeful, but their hearts felt only disappointment and grief that none of them were willing to share out loud.

Tobias's thoughts wandered back to the morning, seeing Pip at the table with Ian, happy and smiling. He'd still looked so sallow and frail, but happy. *When was the last time I saw Pip smile? When was the last time I even paid attention?* Guilt filled his chest and deep regret settled in. *What have I done? When did I become so distant and isolated? When did I become so selfish? I have abandoned everyone!* Anger started to bubble inside him. Anger at himself. *I have let everyone down. Pip, the dragons, my father . . . my father? When did my father become Cornelius? My General.*

There was a pinch in his heart, and he quickly covered it with rationalization. *It was Cornelius who brought us here. It was Cornelius who ordered the murder of the dragons. It was Cornelius's brutality that broke this realm, crushing the spirits of these magnificent beings, and it was Cornelius who took my mother from me. How could one man bring so much destruction to so many lives?*

An unfamiliar loathing brewed in his blood as the realization surfaced. *Because we allowed it,* a voice whispered in his mind.

But before he could identify the voice or begin to sort out all his feelings, Laura's elated voice broke into his thoughts.

"Is that a cave?"

Tobias's head jerked up and panic drummed in his heart. Rosy had led them to Praxton's lair. He hadn't been paying attention; lost in his own disturbing thoughts, he had just let Rosy lead the way. The way she knew. His mind froze, then it raced. *Praxton is not here, he hasn't been here for days.* He took deep breaths to keep him from losing his breakfast, an effect of the intense emotions that moved through him from his previous thoughts: sheer terror, realizing where they were, then sudden relief. It all made him a little woozy.

Ian watched him pale and his forehead bead with sweat. "Tobias—?"

The sounds of soft thumping in the air and snapping of dry branches had them all looking up into the sky. The horses shuffled their hoofs and tossed their heads, neighing uneasily, only to quickly settle as Praxton maneuvered through the trees and gracefully landed in front of them.

***

Pip stared out the big window in the library, the same window Valeen had looked out of a couple days before, where the view encompassed most of the compound and the bare forest surrounding it. *Where could they have gone? What is taking them so long?* His imagination played every tragedy he could come up with over and over again. For the first time in a long time, the loneliness seeped through his bones, settling in his stomach like hot lead. *"You are excused, brother."* Tobias called him "brother." It surprised him that one single word would ignite so much happiness, joy, and hope. *Where are they?*

"Where is everyone?" Cornelius's voice boomed from behind Pip, making him jump. He turned around, his body tense. He glanced over his shoulder and stepped to the side of the window. He didn't like his back against it. Too vulnerable.

"Um, they went . . . on a . . . horseback ride," he stammered.

"What? Alone?" Cornelius boomed again.

Pip cringed. "Um, no, sir. Tobias took them."

Cornelius's face turned red and his fist clenched. "What? Where did they go? Why didn't you inform me? I told you to keep an eye on them, keep them from going into restricted areas! Why do I keep you around?"

Pip lowered his head and began wringing his hands. "I, sir, well . . ."

"Answer me, Pip!"

Brother. Tobias's voice echoed in Pip's head, and in his heart. He dropped his hands to his sides and looked up at Cornelius, meeting his gaze.

"They went into the forest. I didn't think the trees were a restricted area, sir." He was stunned at his sudden burst of courage. A courage he didn't even know he possessed, but it felt good. "They are with Tobias. I'm sure he would not take them to a dangerous place or put them in any harm, sir."

Cornelius could not respond, didn't know how. Pip had never spoken to him so directly insolent. Pip had never spoken to anyone so bluntly.

For what seemed like eternity they just stared at each other, both surprised at Pip's response. Finally, Cornelius found his words.

"Very well. Let me know when they return." He turned on his heel and left the room.

Pip exhaled deeply, unaware that he had been holding his breath. His body relaxed, and he turned back to look out the window and noticed that it looked different outside. He couldn't quite place it, but somehow it appeared less gloomy, less dense. Not so dark and scary. He almost felt he could venture outside and have a look around for Tobias and the others . . . almost.

***

No one spoke, no one moved. They all stared gaping at Praxton, they glanced around at each other, and then all eyes landed on Tobias.

Tobias didn't know what to say. He was relieved to see Praxton alive, and the young dragon still looked strong and healthy, but seemed to have grown even larger. "Praxton, you're alive! Where have you been?" In his excitement to see Praxton, Tobias forgot all about the others and turned to look Praxton in the eyes, softly rubbing the sides of his snout and face.

Tobias? Praxton asked warily into his mind.

"I have been worried sick. You've been gone for days. I'm just so glad you're all right." Tobias continued his inspection of his friend, rubbing and searching down his neck and sides, gently stroking his wings, searching for any injuries.

Ian slowly moved off his horse, not taking his eyes off Praxton.

Um, Tobias—? Praxton thought again.

"We really must work out some way for you to let me know when and if you are going to be out exploring," Tobias continued. "Although I wish you wouldn't, it could be dangerous for—"

Praxton glanced at Tobias, then back at Ian. Not sure what to do, Ian took a step back.

Tobias! Who are all these people?

The echo of Praxton's voice in his head had Tobias quickly turning to face them, remembering the guests he had with him.

"Um, I'm really sorry about this. I didn't mean for us to come this way. Rosy, well, she just knows one way, unless I lead her differently. Don't worry, he won't harm you."

Still, no one spoke for a few more minutes. It was Ian who finally broke their spell.

"He is the most magnificent creature I have ever seen."

Ian took two more steps toward Praxton, and Praxton maneuvered quickly behind Tobias. With his bravado properly placed, he stretched his neck up over Tobias.

"I am not a creature. I am a dragon. And who might you be?" Praxton spoke out loud, stopping the man approaching dead in his tracks.

Ian barked a delighted laugh and turned to look at the others. "Are you seeing this? This is amazing!"

"We're seeing it, baby, now maybe you should come back over here," Laura pleaded.

Tobias raised his arm to stroke Praxton's neck. A smile etched across his face at Ian's obvious pleasure.

"Praxton, these are our friends. They are here to help. This is Ian." Tobias pointed toward Ian, who was standing much closer than the others. "And that is Valeen, Laura, and Luke."

"It's nice to meet you all," Praxton said, feeling safe behind Tobias, even though he was close to a full-grown man taller than the boy.

"Yes, yes, worried. Sick with worry, sad boy," Sabastian chattered as he buzzed between Valeen and Luke, who exchanged a look of amazement.

"Did that bug just talk?" Luke asked Valeen.

"Did you know they could talk?" Valeen responded with her own question.

Luke closed his eyes and shook his head. "Wait, what? The dragons? No, I didn't."

Laura was on the verge of hysterics, not sure if it was pure excitement or terror. "What are the two of you saying? Does everything speak in this place? Should I expect the trees to start up a conversation? Because, you know, I might need to prepare for that."

Valeen and Luke dismounted their horses, and Valeen went to assist her friend, who seemed a bit shaky. Even after Val helped her off her horse, Laura held tightly to the reins.

Luke walked up behind Ian, moving slowly so as not to startle Praxton. "He is beautiful."

At Luke's words, Praxton squared his shoulders with pride and took a step out from behind Tobias so they could all get a better look.

"Yes, yes, very beautiful, and smart and strong. All are beautiful, all, they are," Sabastian chattered with his own pride, landing atop

Praxton's snout and hopping up and down. "Tell them, tell them. Tell them your secret."

Praxton snorted and tried to shake him off. "Quiet, Sabastian," he scolded.

Tobias turned to look at Praxton. "What is he talking about, Praxton?"

"Nothing, the bug is insane, always going on about nothing," Praxton answered, annoyed, glaring at Sabastian.

Sabastian smiled but stayed quiet.

"What is hap-pen-ing?" Laura whispered to Valeen.

Unlike her friend, Valeen was feeling a little giddy. "I don't know, but it's wonderful."

"You can hear that bug talk, right?" Laura asked, skeptical of Valeen's adjective.

Ian leaned back toward Luke and whispered, "That bug is talking."

Luke shoved his hands in his pockets, teetered on his heels, and grinned. "Yes, I hear him. I don't know how or why, but I hear him."

Sabastian leapt off Praxton and began to weave around all of them, stopping abruptly to hover next to Tobias. His eyes darted from side to side, and he zipped back and forth with exaggerated deliberateness. "I am not a bug. I am dragonfly! I am stealthy and I am quick. I am watcher! Yes, yes, I am."

Ian still couldn't take his eyes off Praxton, fascinated and completely enthralled with his beauty and sheer magnificence. It made Praxton a little nervous, and he glanced down at Tobias and then back to Ian. *Why is he staring at me, Tobias? Am I in danger? Should I fly away?*

Before Tobias could answer, Ian hastily stepped forward. "Please stay. None of us will harm you. I apologize for staring. It's just, well, I've just never seen anything so amazingly fantastic as you."

Praxton and Tobias shared a look of shock. In addition to Ian being able to hear his thoughts, Praxton wasn't sure how to take the compliment.

"You can hear him?" Tobias asked.

"You can?" Valeen and Luke asked in unison.

"Hear what?" Laura was beginning to get frustrated. "What are you hearing, Ian?"

Ian turned to look at Laura but pointed at Praxton excitedly. "Him." He barked out another laugh of delight and looked back at Praxton and Tobias. "I can hear him. His thoughts."

Sabastian circled and landed on Ian's shoulder. Ian barely noticed he was there. "Yes, yes, you can hear. Ian and Tobias same, same. Yes, yes, you are guardian!" Sabastian exclaimed.

Ian stepped closer to Praxton and reached out his hand. *May I?* he thought to Praxton.

Praxton reluctantly nodded. Ian was thrilled as a schoolboy as he began to rub and caress the length of Praxton's neck and down his body, closing his eyes, memorizing every spectacular inch. Ian's touch was gentle, soothing, and caring. Praxton felt nothing but respect and awe from him.

"I can feel what he's feeling," Ian said in awestruck reverence to no one in particular.

Valeen, Laura, and Luke exchanged glances.

"Like your horses?" Laura wondered.

"Yes and no. I definitely can get a sense of what my horses need or want. But this is . . . this is clear, there's no interference. It's like our souls are connected." Ian stepped back and gazed up at Praxton. "I know it sounds corny, but it's the most magical thing I have ever felt."

Tobias could only watch the interaction between Ian and Praxton with complete astonishment. At first there was a pinch of jealousy that quickly turned into relief. He was no longer alone.

"Where did he come from?" Valeen asked, stepping a little closer to get a better look.

"I brought him here shortly after he hatched." When no one responded, Tobias lifted a shoulder and continued. "I guess it was an impulse. The General ordered the egg to be disposed of when his mother was . . ."

"Murdered," Ian finished.

Tobias cringed at the word but nodded.

"The General," Luke stated as he too stepped closer.

Tobias nodded again. "I couldn't do it. Lixten was so upset, and I just felt like I should do something, so I kept the egg hidden in my room for as long as I could, then I brought him here. I made sure he ate and taught him what I knew of the dragon ways."

"You taught him to speak?" Luke asked. "So not all dragons know how to talk?"

Tobias smirked. "Well, I didn't think so. But apparently they can, if they want. Mara hasn't ever spoken out loud to me—"

"Who's Mara?" Laura asked as she too came to stand next to Ian, obviously a bit more relaxed.

Tobias exhaled deeply. "She is Ari's sister. One of the few left. Ari is—was—Praxton's mother."

"How does she communicate with you? Mara, I mean." It was Valeen's turn to ask questions.

Tobias shrugged. "I can hear their thoughts, and I can sense their emotions." He hung his head. "I feel what they are feeling, like Ian said."

He looked up at the eager expressions of his guests and continued. "Except it's not their thoughts exactly. It's more like a kind of silent communication. It is how they communicate with each other, but I think for them it's a combination of both sensing and talking in silence, a higher vibration or frequency just between them."

Valeen stepped up and took Tobias's hands in hers. "You hear them, Tobias. Well, you and apparently Ian, which really isn't a surprise at all. But you hear them, and what a blessing that is—for you and for them."

Tobias was taken aback once again by Valeen's magical touch. "I've always been able to hear them. I guess not very many people can; most can't. My mother could, and from what Sabastian has told me, it was difficult for her. I thought I was the only one."

"Yes, yes, sweet Heather, she tried, she did, but no one would hear, nope, no one would hear," Sabastian chattered solemnly, then zipped to a nearby tree and landed on a branch. "There is color, green color, green, see, you can hear!"

No one responded. None of them knew how to respond to a bug, or even if they should. Just talking to an actual dragon was enough for now. But they all noticed the small green shoot of leaf Sabastian was proudly displaying, not understanding the significance.

Ian dragged his sight away from Sabastian and the small green leaf. "What about the others you take care of? Do they talk to you?"

Tobias sighed. "Lixten and Areve had never spoken, out loud or otherwise, to me until just a couple of days ago. I'm still not sure what prompted Lixten, and Areve has been . . . in her Quiet Place for years, since the death of Rem, and, well, as for the juveniles, we just stay out of each other's way. I feel a bit of hostility from them, so I don't spend much time in their lairs."

"The what place?" Laura asked.

Luke wrapped his arm around her shoulder. "I'll explain it to you later."

"And who are Areve and Rem?" Laura was starting to feel a little frantic again. All the suffering and heartbreak that these magical beings and Tobias had endured infuriated her, but she didn't know how to expel it, except to ask blunt questions to try and make sense of it all.

Luke squeezed her tight and kissed the side of her head. "I'm sure Tobias will tell us more, but I think we need to focus on what's in front us right now." He gestured to Praxton, who had stayed quiet, obviously processing all that Tobias was saying.

Praxton felt a pang of sadness at the mention of his mother. What Cornelius had done was almost too much for him to bear. If he thought about it for too long, his blood boiled with fury and revenge. He should be with his father, who was chained to a stone wall; he should have been loved and taught by his mother. The feelings frightened him, the urge to lose control and burn the whole compound down with no regard for the lives he would take . . . then he would think of Tobias and stuff the anger down. Although Tobias rarely spoke of his mother, his heart still ached. Tobias had never brought up Areve either in their conversations, but he knew of her. She was his queen; he could feel the strain of her life force pump through him, but until he'd journeyed to the other place, he had not understood it.

The others did tell me . . . I am part of their tribe, and Areve is our elder. I swore I would never tell. It was our secret. I swore I would keep it locked away in my Quiet Place, where not even Tobias could see it. It was difficult . . . part of him felt like he was betraying Tobias . . .

"Tell them, tell them, should not be a secret, should not," Sabastian chattered in his ear. "They are safe, they are. A guardian, Praxton! Yes, yes, a guardian, same, same. There are others and another." He chattered louder, buzzing over their heads. "Yes, yes, there are others and another."

Nobody knew what Sabastian was going on about, so they all did their best to ignore him.

Praxton let out a breath and slumped his shoulders, the weight of what to do apparent.

"Are you okay, Praxton?" Tobias turned to his friend with sudden concern. "Are you sick? What have you eaten? Where have you been? Is it what I have shared? I'm sorry, but I had to. It is time . . ."

"Tell them, tell them," Sabastian prodded.

Praxton let out another deep breath, his neck and shoulders sinking deeper.

There are others, he thought.

"What?!" Tobias said in shocked disbelief. *What others? Where?* It was an automatic defense to go into silent communication instead of speaking out loud. It was an instinctual protection for himself and the dragons.

"Others?" Ian asked him.

Praxton and Tobias stared at Ian, stunned. Both had forgotten that he could also hear their thoughts.

"What? There are others?" Valeen's excitement vibrated off of her. "Where?"

"Yes, yes, others. Free . . . and afraid. I followed. There is color! And another!" Sabastian buzzed and circled the trunk of the tree, making no sense at all.

Tobias was doing his best to understand everything being said, and who was hearing it and why. "Sabastian, you knew there were other dragons? Why would you not tell me?"

"I did not know. I followed and I found. Lost soul, but I followed and I found. Like Lixten and Areve, thought I heard ghosts in my head. But not ghosts, not! There is color!"

Praxton felt overwhelming guilt that he had broken his promise not to tell anyone about the others, and appalled that he could so easily be duped by a bug. "Sabastian, you followed me?" he asked indignantly. "What were you thinking?"

Sabastian landed on the branch next to the new leaves and lifted his chin. "It is my duty. I am watcher. I am quick and stealthy, yes, yes."

Luke glanced sideways at Sabastian, approaching Tobias and making hand gestures for everyone to calm down. "Okay, let's just start from the beginning. Tobias, tell us about Areve and Rem."

Tobias lowered his head and took a deep breath. "Areve is their queen."

"There is a queen?" Valeen asked.

Tobias studied his feet as he shuffled them on the ground and lifted a shoulder. "I guess she's not a queen in the ruling sense. More of an elder. All the dragons are seen as royalty in their own right. They are all connected by one life force. Areve and Rem were the eldest and sustained the connection. Rem was Areve's mate; he was the first Cornelius killed. That is when the battle broke out. Well, that and the death of my mother on the same day. That was the day everything began to die."

"Yes, yes. Everything and everyone, souls die," Sabastian added sadly.

Tobias looked around at their surroundings and gestured to the bare trees and dry bushes. "Their life force is connected to everything. It took a while for it all to stop growing . . ." He glanced at Praxton and cringed. "Dragons are hard to kill, but Cornelius found a way. Soon everything beautiful was gone, and Lixten surrendered."

He hung his head in shame, unable to look at Praxton or the others. "I didn't know what to do, so I have done my best to just keep those that are left alive—well, those I thought were still alive," he mumbled, looking up at Praxton again.

Nobody spoke, lost in the images of the tragedy that had taken place.

"I'm sorry, Praxton," Tobias mumbled. "I didn't know there were others that fled. I assumed Cornelius and his soldiers killed them all except those who were left at the compound."

"Why Lixten? Why was his surrender the end of the battle?" Ian wondered.

Tobias looked up him and saw what he always saw in Ian's and the others' expressions: compassion and understanding. "He is the oldest male of Areve and Rem."

Ian's rage ran hot through his blood. He glanced at Laura, who had silent tears streaming down her cheeks, and his rage turned to fury.

"I say we find the General and string him up by his balls, jab one of these dead dry sticks into his throat, and let him bleed out slowly."

"Well, thank you, Ian, for that visual scenario, but maybe we can come up with a less violent solution," Valeen told him as she walked up to Tobias, whose face had gone pale, and took his hands in hers.

"Would it be possible for us to meet Lixten?" she asked Tobias gently, pushing calming love into his heart through her hands.

"No, no, yes," Sabastian chirped, hopping up and down on the branch.

"Sabastian, what is wrong with you?" Praxton asked, annoyed.

"Lixten could eat them," Sabastian said matter-of-factly. "Maybe not, but maybe. I will tell him not to." He grinned.

They all looked at each other for reassurance at the dragonfly's statement.

"Sabastian, hush!" Tobias scolded and turned to the others. "I don't think he would eat you," he told them, unconvincingly. "They don't like the taste of us."

"Oh, good, so he could just chew us up and spit us out, is that what you're saying?" Laura rebuked.

Luke chuckled and walked back to Laura, putting his hand on her shoulder. "I think we'll be safe. I don't remember ever feeling hostility from them. And if they can speak and hear our thoughts, then they know we mean them no harm."

Valeen looked up at Praxton but held on to Tobias's hands. "You said there are others? Where?"

Praxton's eyes darted from Tobias to Valeen and back to Tobias.

"It's okay, Praxton, you can tell us," Tobias reassured.

Praxton exhaled. "They are about a day and a half in that direction." He gestured with his head toward the face of a huge mountain in the distance.

"Yes, yes. They are hidden. I followed, I saw, I found," Sabastian chattered.

Praxton moved like lightning and snapped at Sabastian, just missing him and instead snapping the branch he was sitting on in half. "You are an insolent bug. You should mind your own business."

Everyone went still, except Tobias. "Both of you stop it. You're behaving like children and embarrassing me."

To prove Tobias's point, Sabastian landed on Valeen's shoulder and stuck his sticky tongue out at Praxton, who glared back.

Valeen glanced down at Sabastian, who grinned widely back up at her. Something warm and comforting washed over and through her as she smiled back.

"Can you hear what they're thinking, Val?" Laura asked her. "Is that what you heard the other day?"

Tobias looked into Valeen's eyes, still feeling the warm sensation of her touch vibrate through him. "Can you hear them also?" he all but whispered in astonishment.

"I don't think it's the same as you and Ian. It is more like listening to many conversations at once. Not really hearing anything specific. More like an outside observer than a participant."

Tobias nodded, not sure if he was relieved or disappointed. "Okay, I think I understand."

Luke stepped up to Praxton. "How many more are there?"

Praxton glanced at Tobias pleadingly. "I don't know numbers," he finally answered.

Sabastian began to fly in circles again. "Many more, many, grundles and grundles." He landed on the branch next to the single sprouting leaf. "There is color there! I saw, I saw, yep."

Praxton leaned down to Tobias. "I don't know 'grundle,'" he mumbled out the side of his mouth.

"Neither do I," Tobias mumbled back.

Sabastian started pacing the length of the branch, rambling to himself. "They wait for their prince, they wait for their queen. Yep, yep. Queen and prince don't talk to them. They don't know them. They are ghosts in their minds. Yes, yes, only ghost. But not!"

Ian was listening halfheartedly to the conversations around him. He had begun to stroke and rub Praxton again, like he would his horses. It had always been calming for him, and for them.

"Laura, you should come—" he began to say, but Praxton suddenly went rigid and stepped hastily away. Ian froze, not sure if he had done something wrong, wondering if he'd hurt or offended Praxton somehow. Tobias, Luke, and Sabastian also went silent and still.

"What is it? What's wrong?" Laura asked, a little panicky.

Valeen felt a vacuum-like sensation in the air, and the silence that had been present in this place became more deafening. She walked up behind Luke, putting her hand on his shoulder. "What just happened, Luke?"

Luke turned to Tobias. "How many men are still in the compound?"

Tobias dropped his head with a heavy sigh. "Just us. Everyone else has gone on leave or to get supplies."

Sabastian also hung his head. "The time is now," he said solemnly.

"What? Why? What?" Even Valeen was feeling a little frantic as she looked at the confused and concerned expressions of Ian and Laura, yanking on Luke's arm. "Luke, what has happened?" she demanded.

Luke looked between Praxton and Tobias. "I believe the Time Keepers just closed the gateways."

Laura began wringing her hands. "So, what, does that mean we can't leave?"

Luke and Tobias shared a glance. "We have work to do," Luke told them.

Tobias turned to Praxton. "We need you tell us everything you know about the others. No more secrets."

Praxton nodded. "Yes, young master."

Heat rose in Tobias's cheeks and his fists clenched. "I am not your master, Praxton! You need no master."

The shock and dismay on Praxton's face had Tobias immediately regretting his outburst. "I am sorry, Praxton," he told him, reaching up and gently pulling Praxton's head down to be eye level with his own. "I am your friend, I am your brother, I will protect you with all my might— but I am not your master. You are free."

Praxton closed his eyes and let Tobias's words fill his mind and heart. Ian had gone to Laura, wrapping his arms around her in a loving embrace. Luke did the same with Valeen as they all felt the bond between Praxton and Tobias take hold. Praxton's colors became brighter and sharper to vivid orange and indigo. He all but glowed in the drab grayness around them, except for the small green shoots that appeared to have gotten bigger and also more vibrant.

"Val is right. We should probably try to talk to Lixten or Areve," Luke told Tobias. "Do you think they would? I mean, talk to us and not try to kill us."

Tobias smirked. "I don't believe either would try to kill you. How willing they would be to talk to you? Well, that's something else."

Ian stood next to Laura, pulling her close to comfort her. "Well, I think we should head back, then."

Tobias led them through the forest toward the house. The timid uneasiness they felt earlier was replaced with excited hope, even though none of them had any idea how they could possibly help Tobias or the dragons.

Praxton had told them all he knew about the others. They had fled shortly after Lixten surrendered and Areve had retreated to the Quiet Place. In all the chaos, no one noticed them leaving. They were afraid, and their shame and guilt had them blocking and shielding all communications with Lixten and their queen, only communicating between themselves. They had flown until they were exhausted and made a home where they were now. It had taken Praxton a couple of days to get to where they were, and he'd just happened upon them.

"They told me our queen had awoken. I don't know much of our queen, Tobias," Praxton had told him accusingly. Valeen recalled Tobias's sad expression and felt his guilt and pain. Her heart broke a little for him.

Tobias had sent him back to the free dragons, asked him to explain to them what was happening and to wait for Tobias to call him home.

"There is obviously something we're supposed to do, something we *can* do. Why else would the Time Keepers close us in?" Valeen said, asking the question on everyone's mind.

Luke grimaced. "I don't think closing us in is what their intention was, Val. In fact, I feel very strongly that it is to help us, help this realm. We may not be able to leave right now, but nobody is coming in either."

CHAPTER *Nine*

S abastian flew happily through the air, doing zigzags and loops as he went, humming his own made-up song in his head. *We are saved, we are saved. My prince is free, free, we are saved. Areve is awake, we are saved!*

But as he flew through the barred ceiling, he felt rather than heard Lixten's restlessness, and his cheer turned to concern. "Majesty?" he asked, hovering in front of Lixten so he could see both of his eyes at the same time.

"Sabastian, what is happening? Why have the Time Keepers closed the gateways again? Have the Winged Gods come to take us home?" Lixten asked frantically.

"No, no, Your Majesty, there are—"

Sabastian was interrupted by the rattle of Lixten's chains as he lifted his head as close to the opening in the ceiling as he could. "If only I could see the open sky once more."

"Your Majesty—"

"At last I will see my sweet Ari."

"Lixten, hear me!" Sabastian was stunned by his own outburst. But it also stunned Lixten into silence.

Sabastian hung his head. "I apologize, Your Majesty, but listen, listen to your realm, listen to your family." He gazed up at Lixten. "Hear all of them."

"Sabastian, what are you talking about?" Lixten asked, still a bit annoyed at the dragonfly's tone and outburst.

Sabastian landed on Lixten's snout, gripping one nostril with his tiny legs for emphasis. "Reach out to your queen, Lixten. There are others, there are. Hear them, hear them."

Lixten stared cross-eyed at his friend. "What are you talking about? What others?"

"You hear them, I hear them, but like you and Areve thought they were only the haunting of souls. Nope, not. They are real, they are alive. Not ghosts! They are free! Free, Majesty."

***

Pip saw movement in the trees and spotted Tobias leading their guests back home. Thrilling relief filled him, and he ran to the kitchen. *They are probably hungry by now. I'll set out the meat, cheese, and crackers for them as Ruben instructed.* He hastily began tossing the food onto the table, and then it hit him. *They will be leaving soon.*

His heart felt heavy in his chest. *What's going to happen when they leave? I'll be alone again. What if Tobias goes with them? What will happen to me?* Panic and dread swirled in putrid colors in front of his eyes, and he saw himself trapped alone in this house forever, never able to go outside.

Still holding a package of cheese, he leaned against the wall. Suddenly unable to hold himself up, he slowly slid down to the floor. His breathing became erratic and sweat beaded on his forehead. It felt the same as when he tried to go outside, so it wasn't unfamiliar, and he knew that he just had to breathe through the panic. *Breathe, Pip, just breathe,* he willed himself. But this wasn't the same, this was different. There was something else, a loss attached to the fear, an almost unbearable grief.

***

Ian stayed behind with Tobias to help him unsaddle, rub down, and give fresh water to the horses. Valeen, Luke, and Laura ambled in silence toward the house. Their bodies were exhausted, but their minds hummed with anxious anticipation of how they might be able to assist, how they could heal this realm, ideas and solutions spinning in their heads.

Laura's thoughts circled around from fear to excitement to anger and back to fear again. The very real possibility that they might be trapped here made her uneasy, but the hope that they might be able to help these magnificent beings thrummed through her veins. A feeling of purpose she'd never felt before stimulated her nerves. She knew with certainty she had a part to play in all this; she just wasn't sure what that was. *Is this how Val feels all the time?*

"Luke, are we going to be able to leave here?" she suddenly asked, wanting that one circling fear to be put at ease.

"I don't believe the Time Keepers would keep us here. This is not our realm," he assured her as he reached for the doorknob.

When they entered the house, the air felt thick and dreary. They spotted the food on the table but were drawn to a whimpering noise in the corner. All thoughts of dragons and gateways were forgotten when they saw Pip crouched on the floor, his head resting on his knees and a package of cheese dangling from his hand. Laura and Valeen rushed and knelt beside him.

"Pip, what happened?" Laura asked as Valeen took the cheese and tossed it onto the table, then gently wrapped her arm around him, subtly checking for injury. "Are you all right? Are you hurt?"

Pip looked up, looking a little dazed as tears streamed down his face. He couldn't speak, feeling a bit mortified that he had been found in such a state, but when he looked into Laura's eyes and saw genuine concern and . . . love, he let go of the reins of self-control and fell into her arms, sobbing.

Laura cradled him, gently rocking him and cooing soft reassurances. Her eyes locked on Valeen's, searching for an answer. Valeen had none. Her heart just ached for the boy. She stroked his head one last time as she stood looking at Luke with the same silent questions Laura had. Luke gave her the same unspoken answer by just shrugging. They both turned at the sound of the door opening.

When Tobias and Ian came in through the kitchen door, they immediately felt the tension in the air. There was unopened meat and cheese thrown on the table, and in an instant they both froze in their tracks when they saw the concerned and confused expressions of Luke and Valeen. Then Tobias spotted Laura on the floor holding Pip and rushed to her side. "What happened? Did he fall? Is he hurt?"

At the sound of Tobias's voice, Pip released Laura, pushing away from her as he stood, fervently wiping tears from his cheeks. "I'm okay, I just . . . I'm okay," he stammered, putting his bravado back in place. He went to the table. "I put out some food for you. I thought you would be—"

Tobias stepped in front of him, taking him by the shoulders. "What happened to you, Pip? Why are you so upset?"

"Really, it's nothing. I was just—I thought you would be hungry." Pip did his best to avoid eye contact with Tobias and the others, embarrassed and feeling foolish. He just wanted out of the kitchen, away from all these people.

"We came in and found him. I don't know what happened," Luke told Tobias, not willing to let Pip off the hook so easily. The healing of this realm needed to start now.

Tobias bent his head down, forcing Pip to meet his gaze, while still holding him by the shoulders. "Pip, tell me what happened. Did the General do something? Did you try to go outside?" he asked, feeling a little desperate for an answer. While he waited for Pip to process, it dawned on him how much he cared for this boy and how much Pip meant to him. "Pip, you are a brother to me; we are family. I will do whatever you need me to. Please tell me what happened."

Pip gazed a bit defiantly back at Tobias. "Are you going to leave me? Leave me here alone with the General and the . . . dragons?"

Tobias took a shocked step back from Pip. "What? No, I'm not leaving you. I would never leave you." He sighed as a sad frustration moved through him. "The dragons are no threat to you, Pip." He looked around at the others as if searching for a solution. And then it came to him. "We're going to settle this right now." Looking around the room, he spotted a dish towel. "Luke, will you hand me that, please?"

Luke followed Tobias's gaze and grinned, as he knew what Tobias had in mind.

Tobias took the towel. "Pip, I need you to trust me." He turned Pip around, wrapped the towel around his eyes, and guided him toward the door. Ian opened it and they all stepped out, encircling Pip.

Pip's breath hitched as he felt the coolness of the air on his face and the rough ground under his stockinged feet.

"It's okay, Pip; we are all here with you. You are *not* alone. Nothing is going to harm you, I promise," Tobias told him.

Pip swallowed hard and reluctantly nodded. *You are my brother; we are family. I will never leave you.* He brought Tobias's words into his mind, forcing them to circle around his terror. He felt Laura's hand on his shoulder and brought the memories of her holding him so lovingly, the feeling of Valeen's comforting touch, Ian's kindness, and Luke's quiet approvals, all to join in the combating of his fears. He focused on all the feelings of those sensations instead of the discomfort of where he was as they shuffled through the compound.

When they stopped, he heard and felt the others' sudden tension. "It is time. We're going to fix this," he heard Tobias say as he reached over and hit the button that opened the doors to Lixten's lair.

As the doors opened, a rush of stale air washed over them. "Lixten, we need to talk," Tobias said into the darkness. He left Pip and the others standing outside the doors, apprehensive and openmouthed. He went in and began to light the barrels of oil. There was a new determination and purpose in his movements; even though he didn't recognize it, it felt good and right, and he embraced it.

"They are here! They are, they are. There is hope. We are saved, my prince, we are," Sabastian chattered excitedly.

"Hush, Sabastian," a deep, rumbling voice said from the shadows. "The Time Keepers have closed the gateways, Tobias. Do you know why?"

Tobias glanced out the doors at the amazed and startled expressions of his new friends. Pip had gone pale and Ian had his arm around his shoulders, appearing to be holding him up. "I have an idea," he cryptically replied. "Come in, it's safe," he told the others waiting outside.

They all moved together, speechless and awed. Ian and Luke flanked Pip and all but pushed him through the doors. As they entered, Lixten moved out of the shadows. Chains rattled as he emerged into the light, and they all froze in their tracks. In complete disbelief, they all stood where they were, all thoughts racing to comprehend what they were seeing—except Pip, who just concentrated on slowing his heartbeat and trying not to lose consciousness.

Lixten was five times taller and wider than Praxton. He swung his head down to get a better look at them, stopping within a few feet of their heads. "There are others, Tobias, did you know that? And who are these humans? Why have you brought them here?"

"Oh my God" were the only words Laura could muster. Everyone else stayed silent, still not able to form any solid thought at all.

"It's all right, Lixten, they are here to help. And, well, Pip . . ." Tobias gestured to the young boy, who stood rigid, visibly shaking. "He needs to . . . well . . . he needs to know you won't harm him."

"Harm him?" Lixten lifted his head away, offended at the indirect accusation. "Why would I harm him? He has done nothing to me. And why are his eyes covered?" He probed the young boy's thoughts. *Oh, I see, he was witness to the battle,* he thought to Tobias. He leaned in a little closer, squinting as if peering deeper into Pip, and then sighed deeply, shamefully turning his head away. *This boy lives in terror, Tobias. Why would you bring him here?*

Tobias replied in the same form of communication. *His fears are irrational, based on a belief, not a truth.*

Lixten looked back at Pip, searching his memories, and sighed deeply. "I am sorry about your father. I lost mine as well in the battle. The pain and rage can be overwhelming and consuming, I know, but that is all in the past. We can let it go now. I will not harm you. I am not really that frightening, am I?"

"Well, yes, actually you are," Ian said, finding his words. He released his grip on Pip and stepped closer. "Magnificent? Absolutely, but still a bit intimidating."

"Ian!" Laura harshly whispered, trying to grab his arm.

"It's all right," he assured her, speaking over his shoulder and waving his arm behind his back for her to stay where she was.

Lixten looked between Tobias and Ian. *He is a guardian,* he thought at Tobias.

"If you mean by 'guardian' that I can hear and feel your thoughts and emotions, then yes, apparently I am," Ian replied.

"Yes, yes, same, same," Sabastian chattered, landing on Ian's shoulder, grinning widely.

Lixten studied Ian for moment. *What is it you believe you can do? Guardian.*

Ian laughed out loud. *I have no idea,* he thought back.

His laughter made Valeen and Luke relax and also step closer, both exhaling the sudden jolt of surprise they had felt when they first saw Lixten. Laura still wasn't so sure, but amazed just the same. She stayed next to Pip, who was desperately trying to process Lixten's words. There was truth and compassion in them, nothing hostile or barbaric.

He lost his father also. He felt pain and anger? This beast? He didn't sound like the mindless killing animal Cornelius described and warned me about. He spoke to me. Was the General wrong? Was he wrong the whole time? Why would he lie to me, to everyone, like that?

Pip started to feel a little safer now; after all, they were inside a building, and Tobias did close the doors. There was something inside him that began to break away, something he didn't quite understand. It felt like pieces of an illusion he hadn't even known was there. He began to relax and could only focus on what he was feeling, as it occurred to him that his eyes were still covered. *It's amazing what you can see without looking,* he thought.

"You know of the others?" Tobias asked Lixten.

"Yes, Sabastian told me," Lixten replied, glancing at the small insect resting on Ian's shoulder, grinning like a fool.

"Have you spoken to Areve?" Tobias asked.

Lixten hung his head. "I have not. What do I say? I failed her, Tobias."

"You have not failed!" Valeen scolded as she stepped directly under Lixten, craning her head to look up at him.

Lixten's surprise at her outburst and the force at which the words came out made him take a step back. He looked at Tobias, whose expression mirrored his own shock.

Valeen took a step closer, pointing her finger. "What you have done took courage—the willingness to sacrifice everything to stop the death and destruction of your family and home. That is not cowardly; that takes strength, Lixten. There is nothing to gain in dying for a cause that has no rhyme or reason." She was breathing hard as the anger and the sadness overtook her. Something inside told her there was no reason to be afraid, and she stepped even closer. She took a deep breath to steady her rant and spoke calmly. "Lixten, you did what you had to. You are alive, your queen is alive, Praxton is alive, there are others that are alive. There are half a dozen babies that will grow and become all they are meant to be because you did not give up. Surrendering is not a weakness; it is wisdom. Now we just need to set you free."

Lixten glanced around at all the stunned faces of the people around him. Apparently, they were all just as taken aback as he was. He closed his eyes and lowered his head as Valeen's words washed over him and a battle began to rage inside. His mind spun with dignity and shame, with rationalization and guilt. What this woman had just said could be considered disrespectful and offensive, but there was truth in it, and there was no fear in her. Did he make the right choice to surrender to Cornelius? *I had no way of knowing what the General would do. Were his actions really caused by me? Did I have the best intentions for my home and family? Am I responsible for all the death? I just wanted it all to stop, for the humans to leave us all in peace.* All the reasons he'd surrendered to Cornelius came rushing in. He didn't give up. He had thought he was doing what he was supposed to for the good of the realm.

Cornelius betrayed you, Ian's voice said in his head.

It was not betrayal; it was fear. The words echoed through Ian. Lixten and Tobias looked at each other, astonished, searching for clarification. The words were Areve's.

Valeen, Luke, and Laura had no idea what was being said between Tobias, Ian, and Lixten, or if they were even having any conversation at all or just in their private thoughts. Valeen took a moment and decided to get a closer look at Lixten. A line on his neck caught the reflection off one of the lit barrels and intrigued her enough that she stepped even closer. She could reach out and touch the line of folded skin, run her hand along the twelve-inch length of it. *What is this? This is something I can fix, I can heal. We must heal them, Valeen . . .* She was suddenly so mesmerized that she did begin to reach out in an almost trancelike state. *I can heal this . . .*

"Valeen, stop!" Luke ran up to her and yanked her hand away just before she actually made contact.

The sound of Luke's voice got everyone's attention, and they all looked in her direction. Lixten looked straight down at his feet, surprised to see the woman so close, and carefully took a step back.

"What are you doing?" Luke whispered harshly, grabbing her by the shoulders to face him. Then he noticed the glazed and glassy look in Valeen's eyes. "Val?" When she only stared back at him, he shook her gently. "Val, Valeen. Where are you, baby?"

Valeen slowly blinked as if she were coming out of a dream. Then she was completely aware. "What are you doing, Luke? Why do you have a hold of me?"

Luke pointed one finger up. When her gaze followed, her breath hitched. She felt like she was looking up at a skyscraper from its doorway. Lixten loomed above her, his eyes locked on hers. More embarrassed than frightened, she stepped away with Luke's help. "Um, I'm sorry, Lixten, I didn't mean to . . . well, I'm . . . I apologize." She looked desperately at Luke. "I don't know what happened, what came over me." She looked back up at Lixten, who was still trying to recover from hearing his mother's voice in his mind. "Lixten, I am so sorry. I would never intentionally intrude like that."

"It was Areve, Luke. She must have connected to Valeen somehow, was giving her instruction maybe?" Tobias tried to explain but didn't really understand himself. The dragons had never been so . . . forthcoming before.

"We should also talk to her, then." Ian stepped up closer; there was no need to be frightened, and every cell in his body knew it. A small hand touched his shoulder. He turned around to see Pip.

"I think I'm ready to take this towel off my eyes now. These beasts— I mean, these beings are not dangerous. I don't know how I know that, and I don't know why I believed it before. Please, Ian, will you help me?"

"Are you sure, Pip?" Laura asked, gently taking him by the shoulders.

"Yes, ma'am, I'm sure."

"Okay, buddy, here goes." Ian moved behind Pip and began to untie the towel when a glint of reflection caught his eye. "What the hell is that?" He moved Pip into Laura's arms and strode over to the far wall.

"What are you doing, Ian?" Laura scolded, fighting with the knot in the towel on Pip's head while looking over her shoulder at Ian.

"Ouch!" Pip let out a small squeal.

"Sorry, Pip, was that your hair?" Laura asked him halfheartedly, still watching Ian.

"Um, yes, ma'am."

When Ian reached the wall, he began tugging on a thick chain that was apparently bolted to the concrete. "This . . . is . . . so . . . NOT . . . cool! How do we get it off, Tobias? Is there a key?"

"Ian, stop!" Tobias hollered. "There are no keys."

"Areve wishes to speak with us, Tobias, in her lair," Lixten was saying.

"It has to come off. How can we free them?" Ian was breathing hard and sweating but continued to yank on the chain. "They have to come off."

Laura forgot all about Pip and ran over to Ian. "Ian, what are you doing? You're acting like a madman! Stop it!" she pleaded, holding on to one of his arms.

"There is no key, Ian. We will find another way." Tobias was now also pleading.

"Yes, yes, our queen wishes to speak to us, she does, right away." Sabastian began to chatter and swoop in large circles.

"Luke, what is happening here?" Valeen cautiously asked, gripping his arm. He patted her on the hand and stepped away from her to go to Ian.

"Ian, it's all right, everything will be all right." Luke started to cast the soothing spell as he approached. "Ian, it will be all right. We are going to free them. We are."

Ian stopped yanking the chain that he'd draped over one of his shoulders as he pulled with all his might. He fell to knees and put his face in his hands. "No one should be treated this way, Luke. No one and no other being."

"If you men—and women—would kindly move out of the way, my queen wishes to speak with us in her lair. Now." Lixten shifted his body and kicked out a leg. The chain popped off the wall. There was a bit of a slingshot reaction in the chain, and pieces of concrete scattered through the air that had them all hitting the floor. Lixten shook his body and stretched out his wings as far up as they would go, which was less than half their width.

Everyone began to slowly get up, brushing the dust from their clothes. They all stared at each other and then at Lixten, not knowing how to react—except Tobias, who marched right up to Lixten's breast. "You could have escaped a long time ago, and I'm guessing so could the others. Why didn't you?" he demanded.

Lixten looked down at the shocked and confused faces of Tobias's guests staring up at him. "Is there something wrong with your boy?"

"What?" Tobias asked, not understanding the question to his question.

"Pip!" Laura ran to where Pip was still lying on the ground and knelt beside him.

Everyone else followed and circled around the young boy. "Is he okay?" Ian asked.

Valeen and Luke also knelt down to examine Pip for injury. "Did he get hit with something flying through the air?" Luke asked.

Valeen gently caressed Pip's forehead, doing her own kind of scanning for injury. "He is okay. I think he just fainted." She continued to stroke the top of his head. "Pip, wake up, honey, it's all right. Pip, wake up." Her words were soft and consoling as she gently nudged Pip back to consciousness.

Pip's eyes fluttered open, gazing at the concerned faces that surrounded him. He slowly maneuvered up onto his elbows. Confused, he asked, "What happened? Did the dragon get away?"

Ian knelt down in front of him. "No, there is nowhere he needs to get away to. You just fainted."

Pip was mortified. He didn't think he could feel more humiliated than he already was, and twice in as many hours he had lost all control of his emotions.

Laura noticed that Pip had gone paler, if that was even possible, and gathered him up in her arms, kissing the top of his head and softly rocking. "It's all right, sweet boy, I think we all fainted a little." She looked at those around her for support and comfort. "What is going on, Tobias?" she asked vehemently as she pulled Pip closer, tightening her grip protectively around him.

Pip's paleness was replaced with red-hot cheeks when Laura scooped him up, but as he rested his head against her chest, something filled the emptiness he once felt. He embraced and allowed the love to overflow in his heart, into his whole being, and just let it be.

Tobias turned back to Lixten. "That's a good question. Why have you allowed this to go on for so long, Lixten?"

Lixten shrugged a large shoulder. "I vowed that no more lives would be taken—not in my family, not another human, not even my own. What I hoped for did not happen. The General stayed, and as unspeakable as the treatment of the tribe came to be, I could not go back on my word."

Tobias shook his head in disgust. "I just don't understand."

"Besides, Tobias, pulling the chain from the wall is one thing. Breaking through the walls was another thing entirely, and I still had these shackles on." Lixten gestured to the chain around his leg. "Without my fire, I could not get them off."

"You could have killed all of them. You could have let the others defend themselves," Tobias began to rant.

"Yes, but to what end? Our queen had left to the Quiet Place and was vulnerable. I thought I was doing the right thing, the noble thing. But now my queen calls for us."

Ian stood, pulling Laura and Pip up with him. "I heard her too. As polite as it sounded, I don't think it was a request."

"All of us?" Luke asked.

Valeen sighed. "Yes, all of us. I didn't hear her, but I got the feeling all of us were . . . invited."

Lixten swung his neck down within inches of Pip's face. "I will not harm you, boy. You are safe. Do you understand that?"

Pip swallowed hard, and Laura instinctively pulled him closer. "Um, y-yes, mister—sir—yes," he sputtered.

Heat rose in Laura's cheeks in spite of the terror she was feeling. "You are frightening him. Let him figure all this out on his own," she told Lixten hotly, wrapping both arms around Pip.

Lixten peered closer at Laura and grinned suddenly. "You are a good mother," he said, and straightened his neck.

Laura was stunned silent. *Mother? Whose mother?*

"We must go. Tobias, open the door," Lixten rumbled.

CHAPTER *Ten*

Cornelius watched them from the safety of his barred windows as they all went into Lixten's lair, guiding a blindfolded Pip. His thoughts were irrational and tumbled through his mind. *What are they doing? Are they sacrificing Pip? Did they find out he was spying and now offering him to the dragons? They will come for me next. Where are my men?*

He began to pace his room, then stopped to fill his glass of liquor. The bottle was almost empty, but he could not leave to get more. It was too dangerous. *Tobias has turned on me. I was never his father, only the murderer of his mother. He only stayed and took care of the dragons because he was afraid I would kill every last one.* Cornelius smirked as he topped off his glass. *I should have. There would have been enough reason to explain the deed to the elders in the other realms. Where are my men?!*

He moved back to the window and gazed out. *That would have taught the boy a lesson. I should have made him watch as I slaughtered every last one of them. Then he would have never defied me. I may not have his love as his father, but I will have his respect.* He went to take a drink from his glass, which stopped halfway to his mouth when he saw the doors to Lixten's building open.

Tobias stepped out first, searching the grounds, and then waved them out. When he saw Lixten's head emerge from his lair, Cornelius's glass slipped out of his hand and dropped to the floor with a dull thump, leaving a trail of gold liquid across the wooden planks as it rolled under his desk. Lixten slowly lumbered out of the open door. He stood full length, his head reaching past the top of the building as he peered up to the sky. He unfolded his wings that spread out five feet from either side of the building, inspected them while he flapped them slowly, and then, without warning, leapt into the sky and began circling the compound.

Cornelius leaned as far as he could to see out the window to where the huge dragon had gone as the compound erupted in elated shrieks and cries from the other buildings. He backed away from the window quickly, looking around frantically for a weapon, but all he found was a letter opener and a fire poker. With one in each hand, he hastily pushed one of the high-backed chairs and a small table against the door and took cover under his desk with opener and poker in hand. *They will be coming for me . . .*

***

They all followed Lixten out. As sad as it was to see the chains dragging behind him, his reaction to the open air was exhilarating. As he leaped into the sky and flew for the first time in years, none of their emotions could be contained. Happy tears glistened in all of their eyes; Valeen and Laura let them fall. Even Pip was amazed, all his fears of being out in the open consumed by the fantastic scene. They all watched in complete awe the spectacular image and pure joy of a dragon in flight. A sound that was no less beautiful than that of angels singing filled the compound through the tops of buildings, echoing into the blue-gray sky.

The song of dragons, Valeen thought, wiping vigorously at the tears that were blurring her vision.

"We are free, we are free. Saved, yes, yes. Saved." Sabastian zipped through the air, making large circles and weaving in and out around all of them.

As Lixten flew, they followed on the ground, peering up to see where he was going. He had landed atop one of the buildings and waited, his clawed feet gripping the edge, the chains that dangled from his legs clanking against the door. It wasn't just the chains; something inside was thrashing and banging against the door as well.

"Mara!" Tobias said, running to slap the button that opened the door.

Before it could open all the way, Mara lunged out. Broken chains dragged behind her, some of the concrete still attached. *Tobias, what is happening? I heard my mother—she is awake. The gateways closed. Are we in battle? Who are these people?*

Mara, my sweet, it is all right. Tobias walked up to her and began to stroke her long neck. *These are our friends, they have come to assist. There will be no more battles. And Areve wishes to speak with us—all of us.*

Tobias glanced up to where Lixten stood like a regal prince atop her lair. Mara followed his gaze and bowed deeply. *Lixten, what is happening?*

Ian stepped up, still in amazement at the sheer beauty of these beings. Even with their torn wings and faded colors, they emitted unimaginable beauty. *I believe we have been summoned, and what is this lovely dragon's name?* Ian thought, knowing, somewhere inside he could not identify, that this dragon did not speak out loud.

Mara's shocked expression mirrored Praxton's when Ian had spoken to him. *Tobias?* she thought, but not taking her eyes off Ian.

It is okay, Mara, he is a guardian. I think he is just as surprised as we all are. Tobias smiled at Ian. *But he seems to be adjusting quite well.*

Mara straightened, squared her shoulders, and stretched out her wings. She was bigger than Praxton but not quite the breadth of Lixten. *I am Mara, guardian.*

I am pleased to meet you. My name is Ian, Ian told her, giving her a short bow.

Mara then turned to Tobias. *Can I eat him today?*

Ian paled.

No. Not today, my beautiful Mara, Ian heard Tobias tell her. He looked at Ian and chuckled. "She means the General, Ian. Not you."

Mara lifted her head toward the sky. *My queen calls,* she said to Tobias, and in a blink she leapt into the sky.

"Tobias, are you coming?" Lixten asked, leaping into the air, following Mara without waiting for an answer.

"Means what?" Laura asked Ian about Tobias's statement. "What about the General?"

"Mara—that is her name—she doesn't speak like Praxton or Lixten, but I can hear her just the same," Ian told her, gazing into the sky. He shrugged a shoulder and began walking in the direction Lixten and Mara flew. "She asked if she could eat him."

"What? Eat who? Tobias, what is he talking about?" Laura demanded, pulling Pip closer to her.

Pip had stayed quiet, a mixture of old fear and new fascination swirling inside him. He wasn't sure what was happening to him. He just knew he felt safe in Laura's arms. He felt safer around all of them. Nothing could hurt him. Nothing *would* hurt him. He felt protected, and he felt loved. *They must have used some kind of magic. But it's a good kind of magic,* he decided. He pushed away a little from Laura's grip, but not too far away. "I'm okay, ma'am. I see them." *I am safe.*

Laura felt foolish. She was behaving like a frightened schoolgirl, while this young boy she held displayed more courage than she could imagine under the circumstances of how he'd lived. She was becoming very fond of him. She pecked a kiss atop his head. "I know, but I'm still a bit nervous. Do you mind if I hold on to you for a while?"

Pip straightened his shoulders and wrapped his arm around her waist. "Of course, ma'am, I will protect you."

Laura smiled at his sudden bravado and pecked another kiss on his head. *Yes, very fond of him.*

"Tobias, tell us about Mara," Valeen interrupted.

Tobias grinned at her. "We should go too," he replied, and starting walking behind Ian. "Okay. She isn't really dangerous, but she gets riled up easily. She was young when Lixten surrendered. She's actually lucky she wasn't . . . disposed of." Tobias swallowed the lump in his throat that formed with the memory. "Over the years we've formed a special kind of relationship. Mara is very proud and, like I said, easily riled up. I intervened as often as possible and kept the General away from her. I never really worried about him coming to harm from any of the other dragons. But Mara, I think, if given the chance, might just . . . harm him."

"She doesn't speak our language?" Luke asked.

Tobias hung his head and watched his feet. "No, I have only taught Praxton, and, well, that was because that's how I talked to him most of the time. I never tried with Mara. I have always just communicated to her in her language, with thought. That's probably why she responded to me so well."

"So Ian is probably safe," Laura mumbled, then emphasized her words a little louder so Ian could hear her. "Wandering off by himself."

Ian stopped and turned around to face them, sheer delight etched on his face. "Can you feel them?"

"No, but I can see them." Laura pointed to a building set away from the others, closer to the tree line of the forest.

Lixten and Mara landed with a grace and dignity Tobias had not seen in ages. Their colors had brightened and become more defined—still shaded, but brighter—and the only thing taking away from the majestic look of them were the chains that dangled from their legs. Hope and excitement danced in Tobias's heart.

Something in the trees behind Areve's lair caught his attention. Flecks of green and brown spotted the trees and ground. He searched the sky for any sign of the twin suns, but it was still cloudy, not as gloomy, and unless his eyes were playing tricks on him, there was a bluish hue in them. His heart began to race. "That is Areve's lair up ahead," he told the others. Feeling the excitement vibrate through the air, they all quickened their pace.

***

When the noise stopped, Cornelius cautiously crawled out from under his desk. He left the letter opener under the desk, realizing it would be useless, but kept the poker. He hastily maneuvered to the side of the window, took a quick glimpse out, and moved back. He breathed and slowly peeked out. There was nothing, nobody. Lixten's lair door was still open, but there was no sign of the dragon. He searched the sky for movement, not noticing the dreariness that hung in the atmosphere wasn't quite as heavy.

He jumped past the window to the other side to get a better view down the dirt road. He could see the hatchlings' building and where they kept the juveniles, and sighed with relief that their doors were still closed. *What is that boy thinking? It will serve them right if they're torn to shreds.*

He didn't have a good view of the other lairs from this angle; he would have to go downstairs. His stomach growled, but he ignored it and jumped back to the other side of the window so he could see the gateway in the distance. *Where are my men? What is taking them so long? They should have been back here hours ago.*

He studied the area where the gateway stood. There was no shimmering entrance, no defined outline, nothing, only the trees with little green buds. *What is going on? I wonder if I could make it to the gateway—go retrieve my men, and an army. What would I tell the elders? That I lost control, that my own son has been enthralled by the dragons, that I let him spend time alone with them so they had time to poison his brain? I would lose everything.* He slid down the wall, gripping the poker with both hands. *They would banish me to the Uncreated Place.*

"I am a soldier!" he said, gritting his teeth. He crawled under the window once again to the opposite side and peered over the edge of the pane, calculating the distance from the house to the building where the weapons were neatly stacked and the mechanical bow was ready and loaded with a bolt large enough to take down a full-grown dragon. He searched the sky and the grounds again—still no movement. He scanned the trees around the compound—nothing. *Where could they have gone?*

His stomach growled again. This time he wondered how long it had been since he'd eaten, then dismissed it, and began to devise a plan of attack. But his thoughts wandered to Heather, the day the first battle erupted: all the chaos and confusion, all the death. In his mind's eye he saw Tobias, his expression full of fear and shock, and blame. And a younger Pip with his short little arms wrapped around Tobias's neck. Both were staring at him in disbelief and horror. *I didn't stay with him. I left him, and I have stayed gone.*

He closed his eyes and leaned his head against the wall. "My sweet Heather, what did you know? What is it I can't see? There has to be a way."

CHAPTER *Eleven*

They all stopped at the doors of Areve's lair, and a sense of reverence overcame them. Lixten and Mara stayed perched on the edge of the building; the chains around their feet dangled, clanging softly against the building as they waited silently for their queen. Tobias stepped up and hit the button, they all held their breath while the door slowly opened.

A plume of smoke rolled out the open door, and they were assaulted with the smell of sulfur and hot steel. Like a dream, Areve emerged through the smoke. The smoke dissipated into the air. Although she was the same height as Lixten, she was slender in comparison to his bulk. Soft hues of lavender and indigo shimmered down her tall, sleek body. She glanced down at Valeen and the others, gracefully bowing her neck to get a closer look at Valeen. "Welcome to my realm, Miss Valeen. I believe you are the one that awakened me."

Valeen stared at Areve in disbelief. "I . . . it was not my intention . . . I mean, I didn't mean to disturb . . ." *Pull it together, Val!* she scolded herself.

Areve chuckled and pulled back as gracefully as she'd bent forward. "It's all right. I understand." She glanced up at Lixten and Mara, who, in an unspoken understanding, glided down off the rooftop of Areve's lair and landed without a sound in front of her. The emotions that flowed off of them touched the very souls of Valeen and the others, and even though no words were spoken when Areve leaned in and rested her forehead on Lixten's, the communication of love was very apparent. The moment was so tender and true, Valeen could barely contain her own emotions.

Mara stood next to them, reverent and still, until Areve rested her chin atop Lixten's head one last time and, in one dance of movement, lifted one of her wings and pulled Mara under it. Tears of joy and relief fell from Mara's eyes, splashing in small puddles to the ground. Everyone stood quiet, just breathing in the very essence of the dragons' loving reunion.

Areve turned to Tobias, who abruptly began to kneel. She stopped him by nudging him with her snout. "I thought we talked about that,

Tobias," she told him sternly.

Tobias still kept his head bowed. "Yes, ma'am, we did, but I, well . . ." He looked up into her eyes and grinned. "Yes, Areve, we did. My apologies."

Areve turned to Valeen and straightened to her full height, staring down at her. Valeen looked around at the others, feeling a little uncomfortable. Areve said nothing, just continued to stare, as if she were searching for something, like Valeen's very soul was being probed. Valeen glanced at Luke, who was obviously recapturing the pleasant memories of his childhood visit, then at Ian, who was etching every detail into his own memories, and then at Laura, who was holding Pip tight against her, their expressions a little awed and a little terrified.

Areve smiled widely, showing large, razor-sharp teeth. "Welcome to our realm," she said again, then looked toward Ian. *I understand you are here to assist us in reclaiming our home,* she thought to him.

Ian beamed, and thought back, *Yes, umm . . . ma'am?*

Areve laughed out loud. "You too may address me as Areve." She looked around at all of them. "Please, may we not be so formal? You all are our guests."

Valeen was speechless. She was compelled to reply but couldn't come up with anything. She wanted to say how beautiful their home was, how welcome and comfortable she felt here, but couldn't bring herself to speak what she didn't truly feel. It would be a lie and felt disrespectful, so she settled on a simple "thank you."

"Areve, where are your shackles and collar?" Tobias blurted out as he noticed Areve stood free of all chains and steel. He vaguely remembered the smoke and smell of sulfur as Areve came out of her lair. "How? When? How?" he stammered. "The General, he . . . well, I thought . . . I thought he took the fire?"

Sabastian flew in circles around them. "Did not, did not! Areve has fire!" he chattered excitedly, flying in circles and loops around their heads. "Nope. Did not. It was a secret, it was, it was."

Valeen and Luke gave each other a questioning look as well. Valeen glanced at Ian and then back to Tobias, trying to recollect what she'd seen herself, and then to Laura for an answer. Her heart skipped a beat as she saw that Pip had his head buried in Laura's side and she had her arms tightly wrapped around him.

Areve looked down at her feet, scowling, then she looked at Lixten and Mara, whose chains dangled from the steel collars around their necks and the shackles wrapped around their scarred and chafing ankles. A glint of rage ignited in her eyes. "Tobias, would you and your friends please step back?" she asked without looking away from Lixten and Mara. "He did not take my fire!" she said with defiance as she extended to her full height and inhaled deeply.

Tobias moved like lightning, running toward Laura and Pip, all but tackling them to the ground.

Sabastian stopped his prattling abruptly and zipped into the trees out of sight, but before Valeen could wonder what he was up to, she felt the air around them heat up and radiate off Areve. Instinct had her crouching to the ground and covering her head with her arms. She felt Luke stumble next to her, covering her with his own body. Ian saw in his mind, more than he felt, an explosion of searing flames. He took a few steps back but couldn't look away. He watched with fascination as fire erupted from Areve's throat, washing over Lixten and Mara; they seemed to bask in the flames as the scorching heat turned the steel chains around their necks and ankles to liquid, making silver, smoldering puddles that bubbled and seeped into the ground around them.

***

Cornelius stared out the window with shocked terror. Smoke and flickers of flame rose and jumped above the buildings in the distance. How could he explain the horrific deaths of his son and guests to the other realms? How could he ever admit that he lost control, that his own son turned against him, betrayed him? As his thoughts circled for reason and blame, he rubbed his hands over his face and sank once again to the floor. Tears of rage, frustration, and sadness welled in his eyes, but before they could fall, another thought sprang to his mind.

There was fire. How could there be fire? I myself witnessed the severing of the lava canals of the dragons. The queen! Did I take her fire? His mind raced frantically, trying to recall. *She was dormant, not a threat, I was going to get to her later . . .*

"Cornelius, you fool!" he scolded himself. He crept up to peer out the window, fingertips white and gripping the windowsill. Desperately he tried to keep his mind from fracturing and losing all control of his wits. *I am alone, I am a prisoner . . .*

He turned and sat on the floor beneath the window, taking a deep breath. *Think, man, think! How can I escape?*

***

Valeen and Luke stood, brushing the dirt off each other. When their eyes met, giddy excitement rolled out of them in laughter, but it was quickly extinguished when they looked over to where Tobias, Ian, and Laura huddled around a sobbing Pip. They started to go to them, stopping abruptly when Areve moved swiftly in front of them. As she approached where the others were crouched, Ian and Tobias stood and stepped back, hearing Areve's intent in their thoughts.

Laura only pulled Pip closer, burying him into her chest and meeting Areve's eyes with bold defiance. A courage she didn't know she had ignited within her, and she glared up at the eldest of dragons, prepared to defend to the death.

Areve stopped within a few feet of Laura, meeting her gaze. Valeen's blood froze in her veins, her fist clenched at her sides, and she took a step forward. When she opened her mouth to defend her friend, Luke grabbed her arm and pulled her back. "Wait," he whispered in her ear.

Areve caught the movement and turned to glance at Valeen with a subtle warning, then turned back to Laura and Pip dismissively. She closed her eyes and bowed her head. "You have strong instincts. What do they call you?" she asked Laura.

Laura's expression turned to bafflement, and she looked at Valeen, who simply gave her a short nod. Her heart pounded in her chest, but she tightened her grip around Pip, pulling him even closer to her and staring back at Areve. "My name is Laura."

Areve nodded. "May I speak to your young?" she asked with calm sincerity.

Laura's confusion was evident in her scowl. She felt Pip shake his head against her. He had lost all the confidence he had earlier. The abruptness and harshness of Areve's flame had him retreating to a familiar terror in his mind. Laura looked around Areve to where Lixten and Mara sat quietly, watching the situation intently. She looked down at Pip, who had his arms wound tightly around her waist.

"He's not my young, just young." She kissed the top of his head and looked back up at Areve. "And he's scared to death. He has been as much a prisoner here as you have."

Areve nodded again. "I assure you, I mean him or you no harm."

Laura visibly relaxed, letting out a breath of relief, as Ian knelt beside her, resting one hand on her shoulder and the other on Pip's back. "Pip, they will not hurt you," he said softly. When Pip did not respond, he said more sternly, "Pip, look at me." Pip slowly pushed away from Laura, looking up at her. She gave him a reassuring smile.

"Pip, look at me," Ian said again, this time more gently, making sure he had the boy's attention by holding his gaze. "They will not hurt you."

Pip felt his chest fill with courage. He didn't understand how he could be so afraid and feel so safe at the same time. "Okay."

Ian held out his hand for Pip to take. "Okay," he said, pulling Pip up to stand with him and face Areve. He stood behind Pip with his hands on his shoulders. Laura also stood and moved behind Ian, peering over his shoulder.

He's ready, Your Majesty, Ian thought to Areve.

Areve winced at the title. *You're a good man, Ian,* she thought back. *But please call me Areve.*

Ian grinned shyly. "Yes, ma'am," he said out loud, making both Laura and Pip give him a confused look. Ian shrugged. "She asked me to call her Areve."

Areve bowed her head to be eye level with Pip, her gaze locking on his. "See me, child; hear my words. I know the tragedy you have witnessed, I know the heartache from the loss you have felt, and I know the fear that has burned inside you for so long. I am truly sorry for all that you have suffered. Please know I, nor any of my tribe, will never cause you harm. You will always be welcome and safe to walk among us."

Pip felt hypnotized. He couldn't move, could not look away from Areve's piercing eyes. Her words echoed in his heart, and he felt completely safe again. All the doubts and all the dark terror that had lived inside him for so long just seemed to sparkle away. Areve smiled at him and lifted her head to look around at all of them. Pip felt like he was coming out of a pleasant dream, and for the first time in his memory, he saw the incredible beauty and grace of these beings.

"Tobias, will you call Praxton and the others home?" Areve asked.

Lixten and Mara's stunned and sharp looks at him had Tobias staring down at his feet. "Yes, ma'am."

Areve missed nothing. "Tobias preserved a life of one of our own from the indignities and pain we have all suffered. He has also done his best to serve and care for those of us that have been here. There was no disrespect intended, only concern. We owe him our gratitude, not our insolence," she told the dragons with commanding nobility. Lixten and Mara hung their heads in realized agreement. Areve turned back to Tobias. "Will you also, please, release our children?"

Tobias smiled widely. The excitement at the thought of just opening the doors and letting them out had him running toward the buildings where the hatchlings and juveniles were kept while he soundlessly summoned Praxton to return with the others.

He stopped in front of the doors to the hatchlings, consciously aware of not letting the cool air in, and then he felt it: the heat on his back. He slowly turned around to the source and saw one of the two suns breaking through the cloud cover. Even though it quickly slipped behind another cloud, for a moment its rays stretched out like it was awakening from a long sleep. He leaned against the doors for a minute, letting the short burst of sunlight move across his face, before he hastily turned and pushed the button on the building, not waiting for it to open all the way before he ducked through the opening.

He ran to the corrals, where the excited growls and chirps of the hatchlings echoed through the building as they jumped and climbed on the fences. As he unlatched the gates, the hatchlings tumbled out, hopping over and tripping on each other as they scampered out the open doors. Tobias laughed with delight. They obviously knew where they were going. He ran to where the juveniles were and experienced a similar reaction, with a little less tumbling and tripping. Their queen was awake, and they all knew it.

CHAPTER *Twelve*

The intense emotions from the excitement of Areve's fire and conversation with Pip were settling inside Valeen, and the childlike wonder exploded in her mind. *They didn't burn. Lixten and Mara didn't burn when Areve melted the steel chains around their necks and ankles. They seemed to bathe in the heat. How is that possible?* Then she noticed their colors; they somehow became sharper and brighter right before her eyes. *They are indeed the most beautiful beings I have ever seen.*

She then looked around the compound at the concrete buildings that no longer stood out so dominant but looked faded and dull like old ruins. Small green shoots and hints of color had begun to appear through the trees and at the edges of the buildings. A glint of sunlight reflected off one of the windows of the big house in the distance and caught her eye.

"Cornelius!" she blurted out. Everyone turned abruptly in the direction of the house, all expecting the General to be approaching. When they realized that Valeen was only speaking her awareness, a sigh of relief vibrated through them.

"We will deal with him later," Lixten told them with reserved anger.

The sound of chirping and happy growls had them all turning the other direction. The three juveniles ran and flew in a short burst past the hatchlings that stumbled and rolled as they bound toward their queen mother. The sound they made was like a song, reverberating off the buildings and through Valeen's heart. Tobias came in behind them, out of breath.

Areve spread out her wings with a joyful laugh similar to the strum of harp strings as they gathered around her feet, cuddling and nestling against her belly. She encircled them under her wings as she nudged and rubbed noses. They began to push through her feathers, too excited to stay in one place, and she stepped back to let them scatter and race back and forth from Lixten to Mara, who nudged and cuddled much the same way as Areve. "These are your children, Lixten," Areve told him, "your legacy."

Lixten turned away in frustration. Ari was slain for her single egg.

He thought of the other females—what happened to them? He didn't think even Tobias knew for sure, as it wasn't he who'd come to take them away with their eggs. It was another. He just knew he had never seen any that he'd mated with or their eggs again.

Valeen and the others watched the dragons in sheer delight, the gentleness and tenderness they expressed almost contradictory to their size and capabilities . . . and the rumors that had haunted them for centuries.

As Tobias witnessed the encounter of the young and the adult, shame burned in his belly. *How could I have kept them isolated from each other? How could I have allowed it? They are a family, a loving, caring family, and I kept them separated. And what of their mothers? What atrocity had I looked away from?* The feeling of self-loathing and disgust all but overtook him, and with his head hung low, he began to step away from all the happiness.

He was startled by a hard push in his back, and when he turned, he was staring into the deep green eyes of Lixten. *You are not to blame, Tobias* was all he heard, then Lixten nodded sharply and turned away, leaving him standing there both surprised and pondering Lixten's words.

"They're like puppies," Pip whispered to Laura with quiet surprise. The sound of his voice had the hatchlings stopping and peering in his direction. He went rigid as, in one force, the hatchlings ran, jumped, and tumbled toward him. They jumped up and down on his legs, vying for attention. He relaxed a bit when Valeen and Laura knelt down and began to pet heads and rub bellies. When he determined they were no threat, just like puppies, he reluctantly knelt next to them, cautiously reaching out to touch and rub heads and ears as Valeen and Laura did.

It was an instinct of the young knowing the young that had the hatchlings gathering playfully around and bouncing off Pip and each other, licking and gently nipping at his hands and face, and each other's, until they knocked Pip off his feet. Laura felt a pang of fear for him until she heard his giggle escape from the pile of baby dragons.

"All together, all together, same, same, happy, all happy again. There is color, there is suns, all happy," Sabastian chattered above them, doing the familiar loops and circles in the air. Laughter erupted from Pip as the hatchlings jumped and snapped at Sabastian.

Areve gave a satisfied nod toward Pip and the hatchlings, and turned to Lixten and Mara. *We have work to do.*

Both Tobias and Ian looked up quizzically at her.

Our realm is still replenishing. It could take years to rebuild our home. And we have no fire, Lixten replied heavily. Tobias stared down at his feet with that familiar pinch of guilt in his stomach.

Those barbarians cut it out of us! Mara thought, taking a step forward. Her head was lowered, her eyes fiercely pierced and focused in the direction of the house as her wings aligned with her body in a defensive, battle-ready stance. The juveniles followed suit, mimicking her form. *I will be happy to rid our home of that man. Tobias should have let me eat them all!*

Luke stepped up and put his hands on Valeen's shoulders, ready to defend. Tobias went rigid, and Ian squeezed Laura tightly against him. The hatchlings and Pip abruptly stopped their play. The hatchlings ran under nearby bushes that were just starting to bud, and Pip moved to crouch behind Ian and Laura as they all felt the shift of energy and sudden heat in the air from Mara. Even Sabastian went silent and stilled as he landed on Tobias's shoulder.

Areve stepped in front of her and touched her forehead against Mara's. *The time for bloodshed is over. He is only one man. We will find another way.* Her response was calming and one of authority. Mara grudgingly retracted her stance, and again the juveniles followed her lead, and shamefully hung their heads when Areve glanced in their direction.

Valeen exhaled heavily when she saw Tobias close his eyes, lean his head back, and drop his shoulders in relief. Ian's response was almost exactly the same. The gesture alone had Laura and Pip also breathing easier.

Luke stepped over to Tobias. "What the hell was that all about?" he asked in a hushed voice.

Tobias shrugged, more to slough off the tension than to seem unconcerned. "Mara wants to eat my father, but first she would like to disembowel him." He couldn't help but chuckle at Luke's shocked expression, and he slapped a hand on Luke's shoulder. "It's okay, though—Areve won't allow it," he told Luke, still grinning.

Valeen found her courage and turned to Areve. "Now what? Have the Time Keepers opened the gateway?"

Tobias and Luke shared a look with Lixten and then looked back to Valeen.

"No, they haven't," Luke said, a little more hotly than he intended.

Laura stepped away from Pip, leaving him distracted with the hatchlings that also seemed to feel the 'all-clear' in the air and resumed their play with the boy. "What does that mean? Are we stuck here? I mean, I like the place and all, but I really want to go home soon."

Ian sauntered up next to Valeen. "What about Cornelius?"

Areve positioned herself to face all of them. She stood with regal grace that captured the attention of all parties. "We should all rest and eat. It's been a busy day, and emotions are high; any decisions made now would not serve us." She leveled her gaze on Valeen. "We have things to do, and I think you can assist." It was all she said before she unfurled her wings, lifted off the ground, and flew into the trees. Lixten and Mara followed.

The dragons' takeoff caused plumes of dust and debris to whirl around Valeen and the others. They covered their heads and faces with their arms, but none were willing to look away as the spectacular beings took flight. The younger dragons and the hatchlings scrambled behind them on foot into the brush.

They all waited in silence until the dragons were but fluttering specks in the distance. Pip's stomach growled, making him blush when they turned and looked at him.

Ian put a hand on Pip's shoulder for reassurance. "Areve—and Pip's stomach—are right. We need to eat and rest. It has been a busy day, and I don't know about all of you, but I can't seem to keep a straight thought in my head."

Luke took Valeen by the hand. "I could eat. What we got in the kitchen, Pip?"

Pip shrugged. "There's still the meat and cheese I was getting out earlier, but it's probably warm by now."

"Well, let's see what we can do," Laura said, brushing the dirt from her clothes that was left from the wing wind of the dragons.

Ian was right. Valeen couldn't get a straight thought to settle in her mind either. She had so many questions. *Where is Praxton? What about the other dragons? Can they speak also? What is the gift that Tobias and Ian share? Where is Sabastian? What happened to Tobias's mother?* That might be a question for later, she decided.

***

As they all strolled back to the house, Valeen and Luke held hands while Luke kept studying the sky. Laura and Ian flanked Pip, each resting a hand on one of his shoulders. His stockinged feet were covered in dust and bits of straw that clung determinedly. And Tobias sauntered behind them, occasionally looking back over his shoulder with a small, satisfied grin etched on his lips.

Sabastian zipped around and between them, humming happily. Tobias was happy again, like he was when he was just a child. *No more death, no more.* He deliberately fell behind the small group to contemplate what was going to happen next. It was his job to study, to learn, to watch and listen. *Their wings are free, but not their hearts. New friends to assist, the Time Keepers brought them, they did, they did. The others will come, come home. They will have their home.*

Sabastian thought more on the other dragons. There was still mistrust and fear, he knew, and a tingle of concern shivered down his body.

***

Cornelius heard muffled voices outside the house. He rested the back of his head against the wall and closed his eyes. *Thank the gods, my men have returned.*

He went to the door to leave, already devising a new plan of attack, but the sound of a woman's laughter had him freezing with his hand on the doorknob. He listened more closely, leaning his ear against the cool wood. He heard the soft giggle of a child and then Tobias's voice. Surprise and confusion had his thoughts tumble into irrational conclusions. *They are all dead. I saw the fire. They have come back to haunt me! Come back to lure me out.* His heart started to pound in his chest and sweat beaded on his forehead. *What do I do? How do I stop a ghost?*

He looked down at the fire poker still in his hand, and rage ignited from sheer terror. He tossed it across the room, knocking over and shattering a glass lamp as it hit the floor. *I can still defend myself.* He pushed himself off the wall. Irrational thoughts swam in his head as he picked up the poker and retrieved the letter opener and sat in front of the fireplace. With the poker in his lap, he began the slow and deliberate strokes of the opener on the stone mantle of the fireplace. The scraping sound was soothing.

***

Luke opened the door to the kitchen, holding it open for everyone to file in. They were hungry, dirty, and exhausted. But even in the

112

exhaustion there was a hopeful excitement. Nobody knew the answers to what to do next, but the idea that there was in fact a possible solution made them a little giddy.

"I dibs first shower," Laura announced.

"I dibs second," Luke hastily said.

Valeen looked at Ian and Tobias. "I guess that leaves food up to us."

"No way," Ian told her, grabbing Laura around the waist and dipping her backwards, making her squeal out in laughter. "I think this lady might need some watching over from this guardian." Pip giggled at the spectacle.

"Pip and me can handle a meal if you guys would like to get cleaned up," Tobias told them, nodding in Pip's direction. "Pip, why don't you get some clean socks on and wash your hands, and we can put something together for our guests."

Pip smiled widely and ran through the door that resembled a closet down to his rooms.

Ian sighed deeply. "That's still a disturbing illusion. You should do something about it, Tobias. Find him a decent room."

"I will. Now leave us. I really want to do this one thing for all of you," Tobias said.

"Should someone check on the General?" Valeen asked casually, taking Luke by the hand to lead him out of the kitchen. When everyone just stared at her, she shrugged a shoulder and changed the subject. "Well then, I guess we'll leave you to it, Tobias." She stopped in the doorway and turned. "Thank you, Tobias, for everything," she told him sincerely.

Tobias didn't know how to respond, so he just nodded and went to the sink to wash up.

After everyone went to their rooms, Tobias and Pip moved silently through the kitchen. It was a comfortable silence, each in his own thoughts. Pip felt proud and safe, and something else he couldn't quite identify, but it felt warm and comfortable, like a cozy sweater. *Maybe I could draw this feeling, give it shape and color. Give it a name. Create a special place I've never been before.* A soft giggle bubbled out of him. *I've never been to any of the places I've drawn. Would Tobias take me on new adventures now that I can go outside?* The idea made him giddy, but a second thought dissolved the happy excitement, turning it into bitter fear. *Would the General let me leave?*

Tobias pondered Valeen's concern for the General. It made no sense. He set out plates and silverware, oblivious to the shift in Pip's demeanor. *I don't understand—how could they have any concern for a man who caused so much pain and suffering? 'He's afraid.' Areve told us it was fear. How is that true?* Tobias wondered. He had never perceived his father as anything but fearless, and cruel.

He would go to his father's rooms, a part of the house he'd always avoided, and invite his father to have a meal. Feeling his own kind of fear that resembled resentment, he went about preparing a meal for his guests.

CHAPTER *Thirteen*

Valeen sat cross-legged on her bed, doing her best to block out the visual assault around her while she towel-dried her hair. Luke lay beside her with his hands on his chest, staring up at the ceiling. She dropped the towel heavily in her lap and sighed. "What are we supposed to do, Luke?"

"What do you mean? We're supposed to eat and rest, and not necessarily in that order," he told her humorously, still staring up at the ceiling.

Valeen threw her towel at him, making him flinch and lean up on one elbow to face her. "That's not what I meant and you know it. I don't know what else we can do. It's obvious that all Tobias had to do was open the doors and Areve just had to wake up, or come back, or whatever. So do you think it was some kind of catatonic state she was in? You know, from all of the trauma she's endured? I mean, why are we trapped here? I'm starting to get a little homesick, and not being able to leave at will is a little unnerving."

Luke could only stare at her for a minute, blinking. He knew how her mind worked, but it still took any rational being a moment to catch up. "Which of those questions would you like me to address first?"

Valeen covered her face with her hands and growled, flopping back on the pillows. "I guess it's safe to assume the Time Keepers haven't opened the gateways yet." She squinted sideways at Luke. "You'd tell me, right?"

Luke also fell back onto his pillows to stare at the ceiling once more. "Okay, we'll start backwards. Yes, I'd tell you, although I think you would know as much as any of us. You're still connected to the magic, maybe even a little more in other realms than at home. That's a no, by the way: The Time Keepers haven't opened the gateways."

Valeen nudged him in the ribs with her elbow, making him grunt out a chuckle. "Okay, what was next? Oh, right, I guess it could be considered some kind of . . . what did you call it? . . . catatonic state, but the Quiet Place is more a place you choose to go to recharge and resolve. You're not forced to stay there, like the place where Mary was last spring, but you can get too . . . comfortable, and get lost," he told her, referring to the void Mary was sent to when she was attacked by a rogue Time Keeper.

He leaned up to face her, resting a hand on her bare thigh. "That's nice," he said, smoothly caressing her skin. "So, where were we? Right, I believe there is a bit more to it than just opening the doors to their lairs. I think a series of circumstances needed to happen, and one of those circumstances included us. They needed someone on their side, like a support group such as it is. And lastly, I have no idea how we're to assist. I suppose it will come to us when the time is right. I believe on some level we all agreed to be here in whatever capacity we could."

Valeen leaned up on one elbow to face him. "What if we're stuck here for years? I mean, I—we have a life back home."

Luke mirrored her position, leaning up on one elbow again, casually tucking a strand of her hair behind her ear. "I don't believe it will take quite that long. Besides, it has only been about a day and half we've been gone from home."

Valeen stared at him openmouthed, making him chuckle. "You'll see, it will all work out," he told her, then softly kissed her still-open mouth before he fell back onto the pillows, resuming his stare at the ceiling. Another thought occurred to him, and he smiled widely. "Wait until both suns come out and night never comes. That is an experience in itself."

He glanced sideways at her and could not stop the laughter from rolling out of him at her expression as she desperately tried to work it out in her mind. He reached out and patted her bare thigh. "It will be okay, my love, just another adventure." He rolled back up onto his side, his hand resting on her thigh. "This is nice," he said again, and began to gently stroke her soft skin. The gesture had her attention coming back to him, and he watched as her eyes changed to that color of storm clouds.

"Why don't we just forget about all this for a while?" he said suggestively, kissing her softly on the mouth. Valeen went soft inside. She let her thoughts and feelings dissolve in Luke's arms, and without another word, they released the excitement and tension of the day through each other.

***

When Valeen and Luke entered the kitchen, they immediately inhaled the scent of warm bread. Tobias and Laura were setting out bowls and glasses on the table. Laura glanced up at Valeen. "Did you enjoy your nap?" she asked her with a knowing glint in her eye.

Valeen snatched an olive from a bowl on the table and popped it into her mouth. "Yes, very much, in fact, thank you for asking," she replied, shooting a smile at Luke, who busied himself at the counter, helping Tobias pour a fabulous-looking soup into a large serving bowl.

"Where did Ian get off to?" Luke asked absently, slipping an oven mitt on his hand to retrieve the rolls from the oven.

"He went down to Pip's room. He insisted on seeing Pip's drawings," Laura told him as she studied the wine before setting it on the table.

"Should we put some aside for Cornelius?" Valeen wondered out loud again.

And again everyone stopped what they were doing. Tobias was jolted out of his thoughts at the mention of his father's name. And again Valeen looked around at the blank faces staring back at her. "What? The man has to eat."

The silence in the room broke when Ian and Pip clamored through the doorway. "Laura, you have to see—" Ian was saying, then went still as he walked into the tension of the room. "What'd I miss?"

Luke patted Ian on the back, releasing some of the tension. "Nothing. We were just wondering if the General wanted to join us for a meal."

"Well, I don't know that I'd go that far," Valeen began, defending her idea.

"The man has to eat," Ian agreed, then sighed, "even if he is as crazy as a loon."

Valeen gestured toward Ian. "See?"

Tobias went about setting the table, pondering the statements in silence. But his thoughts were interrupted by the sound of Pip's timid voice. "I don't bother the General when he's in his rooms."

Valeen and Laura shared a disgusted look of rage that this young boy had lived in such fear and loneliness for so long. Valeen began to rethink her concern about the General. *What does that say about you, Val?* she thought. Not wanting to let her own fear or anger take hold, she bent down to Pip, tucking a finger under his chin. Gently lifting his head, she smiled warmly at him. "It's okay, we'll just put some aside for when he decides to come down."

"I'll go," Tobias blurted out. When everyone turned to look at him, he shrugged a shoulder. "After we all eat, I'll take him a tray. I think we're long past needing to have a conversation."

While they ate, they talked softly amongst each other, going over the day's activities, reminiscing about other adventures and what it was like back home. An occasional giggle bubbled out of Pip while he talked with Ian, but Tobias stayed especially quiet, letting out a small chuckle or grunt when he was brought out of his thoughts. He was desperately trying to put his thoughts and feelings together about his father. *Have I ever known real love for the man? Was it respect or fear that kept me here so long, doing his unspeakable bidding?*

In the vision of his mother falling backward over the balcony and Cornelius standing there looking down over the edge, there was a vague recollection of Pip standing next to him. It all floated through his memories in slow motion. He never saw her again; he couldn't recall a burial. *What did my father do with her body? Where did the bodies of all the dragons go? Did he push her? Is that what I saw?* In his heart, he couldn't imagine that even his father would be capable of such an act. But after witnessing the pain and cruelty inflicted upon the dragons in the following years, he wasn't so sure.

There was so much rage in his being. Had he believed his own father could have murdered his mother as easily as he'd murdered so many dragons? He had never allowed the questions to surface and definitely would never have voiced them. He had buried every emotion he felt the minute his father walked past him and Pip huddled together on the floor. *When was it exactly I began to push Pip away? Where have I been? 'The Quiet Place.'*

He was mildly surprised when he looked up and was standing in front of his father's door holding a tray of warm soup and bread he vaguely recalled preparing. Did he say something to Luke and Valeen? Even the walk was distant and automatic in his mind. Well, it didn't matter now; he was here. He took a deep breath and knocked on the door. "Father, I brought you a meal."

He hung his head and sighed when there was no reply. He waited a few moments and knocked again. "Father, we need to talk."

The door snapped open and an arm reached through the gap, grabbing Tobias by the collar, yanking him over the threshold. The tray of soup and bread toppled out of his arms and clattered to the floor.

Cornelius pulled Tobias in and pressed him up against the wall with one arm across his chest. He put the sharpened blade of the letter opener to his throat as he kicked the door closed, taking his arm off Tobias's chest long enough to turn the lock but not moving the blade.

***

Valeen stared out the big bay window in the library, the scene around her similar to when they'd first arrived: Luke sat in a chair deep in his own thoughts; Laura was on the couch, her head leaned back and her eyes closed. The difference was Ian, sitting on the floor head to head with Pip, looking over the boy's drawings. Pip was enthusiastically explaining them to him. He looked like the sweet, happy young boy he truly was, instead of the scared, withdrawn, and haunted-looking boy they'd first met, not even a whole week ago. The excitement of the day and full bellies had them all feeling sated and sleepy.

Valeen studied the view outside the big window. Everything looked and *felt* different. The doors of the buildings in the distance now stood open, looking dark and hollow. The air wasn't as damp and dreary, and the atmosphere had taken on a soft yellow hue. The new scenery fascinated her. The gray dullness that was there just this morning had morphed into sprigs of green shoots and small bursts of color that scattered across the compound and through the forest. *What powerful magic,* she thought.

"It is at that," Luke said, coming up behind her and resting his hands on her shoulders.

Valeen scowled up at him. "I'm still not sure if I'm okay with you reading my thoughts like that or not."

Luke just smiled at her and kissed the top of her head. Then a thought occurred to Valeen. "Why is it you can read my thoughts and not the dragons'? And what about everyone else? Can you hear Tobias's or Laura's thoughts?"

Luke rested his chin atop Valeen's head and stared out at the view like her. He smiled to himself; the memories of what it looked like when he was a boy were surfacing to life as he contemplated his answer. The sky was a soft lavender and the clouds were golden-lined as they separated and drifted silently through the air. "Well, I can't really read your thoughts as they are. We've just known each other for, well, some time now, and our souls have been so intertwined, it's more of a special kind of connection."

Valeen chuckled at the thought of them knowing each other for hundreds of years. Even though she could not recall all of them, apparently Luke could. It was still baffling and mind-blowing to her, but after all she had experienced in the last eighteen months, it wasn't quite as unsettling.

"As far as the dragons—" Luke began, but the sound of crashing dishes from up the stairway stopped him from continuing. They all jumped up and looked at each in shock.

Laura hastily grabbed Ian by the arm. "Tobias took Cornelius food," she told him fervently.

Luke looked at Pip. "Where are the General's rooms?" he asked.

"I'll show you," Pip said as he ran to the stairway.

Ian grabbed his arm and stepped in front of him before he could ascend. "Wait, stay behind us."

Pip nodded and stepped behind Ian. "His rooms are up on the next floor, to the left." He pointed.

Luke and Ian took the stairs two at a time. Pip, Valeen, and Laura followed.

When they reached the top, Luke peered around the corner and down the hall. "Tobias?" he called out. When there was no reply, he glanced back at Ian and the others' concerned expressions. "Tobias, is everything all right?" he called again. Still no answer.

Ian made eye contact with Pip, asking the question without speaking.

"It's the last door on the left," Pip whispered.

Luke peeked around the corner and saw the broken bowl and spilt soup and bread on the floor just outside one of the doors. "Okay, you three wait here," he instructed. "Me and Ian will go have a look." Tentatively, he and Ian stepped up to look down the hall.

As Luke and Ian slowly started to walk down the hall and disappear from sight, Laura leaned into Valeen, putting a hand on her shoulder. "Cornelius wouldn't harm his own son, would he?" she whispered.

Valeen felt like she'd swallowed hot lead. She looked at the faces of her friend and the young boy standing next to her, and, without responding, followed Luke and Ian down the hall, Laura and Pip right behind her, ignoring Luke's instruction. When they came shuffling quietly up behind Ian, he scowled at them but said nothing. Luke didn't seem surprised at all that Valeen did not heed his warning and only gave them a passing glance, then softly knocked on the door.

"Tobias, is everything okay?" There was no reply. "General, are you all right?" Still nothing. He leaned his ear against the door and thought he could hear muffled voices. He tried the doorknob. "Locked," he mouthed to the others huddled around him.

He heard Tobias cry out, then the sound of shuffling and grunts on the other side. Without thinking, he took a step back and kicked at the door. There was the sound of wood splintering, but the door didn't budge. Sounds of something tipping over and glass breaking had both Luke and Ian ramming the door with their shoulders. Valeen and Laura moved back against the wall, pushing Pip protectively behind them. On the third run, the door gave. Pieces of wood scattered through the air. Valeen and Laura stooped down, covering their heads with their arms and covering Pip with their bodies, as Luke and Ian stumbled into the room.

Cornelius was straddled over a stunned and bleeding Tobias, his arms raised above his head with the letter opener gripped in his hands, ready to plunge into Tobias's chest.

"No!" Luke yelled and leaped onto Cornelius, wrestling him to the floor. They grappled across the floor into a fallen table; Luke hit the back of his head on one of the corners and fell onto his back, where tiny shards of broken glass bit into his skin, causing him to cry out.

Valeen, Laura, and Pip ran into the room when they heard Luke shout. Their first sight was of Tobias lying on the floor, bleeding from a gash on his neck and a trickle of blood running down his chin from a split lip. All three ran to him. Valeen clamped her hands over the wound and watched in horror the unbelievable battle that ensued just across the room.

Cornelius regained his footing first and began approaching Luke, who was still staggering to his feet. Ian saw the madness in Cornelius's eyes and lunged, but the girth of the General kept them from falling to the floor. Cornelius swung his elbow back, hitting Ian in the jaw; he felt like he had just been kicked by one of his horses.

Cornelius spun around, swinging the blade as he turned. Still feeling disoriented from the blow, Ian tried to jump out of the way, but his reflexes were too slow. The blade sliced across his chest. A line of blood gushed through his torn T-shirt. Cornelius forgot about Luke and moved toward Ian.

Pip appeared beside Valeen and held out a towel. "Here, use this," he said, thrusting it at her. Valeen's first thought was *Where did he get a towel?* Another yell and grunt from across the room caught her attention just in time to see the blade Cornelius was holding slash across Ian's chest.

"Let's sit him up." Laura's voice was distant at first, but a moan from Tobias had her refocusing on her task. She took the towel from Pip, pressing firmly with one hand, and used all her strength in her other arm to assist Pip and Laura as they heaved Tobias up to a sitting position.

The sting of the blade and the shock of seeing his own blood on his hands had Ian frozen in disbelief as Cornelius moved toward him. "Ian!" Laura's voice vibrated in the back of his mind, then he saw Cornelius hit the floor in front of him as Luke tackled the General around the legs.

Cornelius felt a sharp snap in his knee, and then pain and color exploded in his head as he hit the edge of a windowsill on the way down. The letter opener dropped and skidded across the floor.

Unable to stand any longer, Ian fell to his knees, doing his best to not lose consciousness, but it felt like a losing battle. The adrenaline running through him had his heart pumping the blood out of the cut on his chest, and he felt lightheaded. When he looked up, he saw Luke kneeling in front of him. His hand was pressed against Ian's chest, blood oozing through his fingers. *Is he saying something?* Ian couldn't focus. His jaw was throbbing, and a bitter copper taste filled his mouth.

Then Laura was beside him. She was crying. Her face started to blur and fade away. "Ian, stay with me! Ian!" Her words were a faraway echo. He could feel himself falling. His last thought was of the softness of her lap as he drifted into blackness.

Cornelius clambered to his hands and knees, but his injured leg wouldn't hold him, and he fell against the wall under the window. The room was full of people crying and bleeding. His knee was screaming, and his head was pounding; he gingerly touched the side and drew back bloody fingers. Confused and disoriented, he tried desperately to make sense of it all.

There was a woman sobbing over a lifeless man. Another man sat next to her, talking softly. He glanced to the other side of the room and saw Tobias sitting on the floor, Pip kneeling beside him. *Tobias?*

His thoughts suddenly wound tightly and sharpened, and he saw those two young boys holding on to each other, watching in terror as Heather fell. He shook the memory away, and it all came rushing back. His guests, the dragons, the spell-cast ghosts come to claim him!

He pushed himself up, using the wall and windowsill as leverage. He spotted the letter opener on the floor. It was sheer will and terror that forced his body to move. As quickly as he could he limped toward the door, scooping up the opener as he ran out. No one followed.

CHAPTER *Fourteen*

Sabastian watched in terror through the window, his tiny legs gripping the pane. *Madness, horror, madness! I must get help, I will find Areve!* He jumped off the windowpane, aimlessly flying as fast as he could through the compound. *His mind is broke, broke! Yes, it is, it is!* He buzzed in every direction, not knowing where to look first.

Stop, stop. Stop! he told himself, hovering in the air, then slowly gliding down to the ground. *Think, think, Sabastian. Think! Where did they go?* He looked in the direction of Lixten's lair. *No, no, no.* He hopped a couple of times in the direction of the hatchery. *No, no, no. Where? Where? Was not watching, was not.*

The door to the house banged open, startling Sabastian. He went very still and turned the color of the ground. To his surprise, he changed to a green-brown color instead of the gray-brown he was used to. For a fleeting moment, his heart filled with hope.

Then he saw the General half running, half limping out the door, wildly searching the skies and gripping the sharpened letter opener tightly in one bloody hand, heading down the pathway toward the gateway. Sabastian watched him stumble and fall, crying out in agony, then scramble quickly to his feet again. Cornelius's clothes were torn and spattered with blood, his head bleeding, his face sweaty and dirty, tears streaking through the dirt and grime down his cheeks.

As Sabastian observed Cornelius, a sudden deep sadness filled him. He could never really read the General's thoughts, but this was something else. There wasn't the barrier of hate and rage. It was a whirlwind of emotions and random thoughts that made no sense. Sabastian hung his head. *So lost. So, so lost. So sad, yes.* He looked up and saw Cornelius leaning his head against the gateway, banging his fist against it and sobbing, then turning and running into the trees. *So sad, so lost . . .*

The others! Yes. Lixten and Areve went to catch Praxton and the others! He leapt into the air excitedly and zipped in the opposite direction of where the General went. *Yes, yes, the others!*

***

Valeen pulled on the deepest part of her magic. Even though her mind felt frozen in horrific disbelief, she drew on every resource within her that she knew of and lit up the room in healing light. She knew she didn't have the power of the Sun People but did have enough to slow the bleeding from Tobias's neck and surround those she'd come to love with the magic that had been allowed to surface. But still, she could only watch helplessly as Luke and Laura knelt beside Ian, not knowing what condition he was in or how severe his injuries were.

"I don't know what happened, I don't understand," Tobias suddenly said distantly, putting his hand over Valeen's as she gently touched the cut on his neck, then dropped it back into his lap. "It makes no sense, he was making no sense."

Valeen looked at Pip. His face was streaked with silent tears as he held on to Tobias and watched Laura and Luke across the room, obviously torn as to where he wanted to be. Valeen knew exactly how he felt. "Pip?" she said, trying to get him to focus. "Pip, do you have any medical supplies?"

Pip turned and looked at her, confused and frightened. "What?"

"Bandages, tape, things like that. You know, medical supplies?" When Pip just stared at her, she took his hand in hers, forcing him to concentrate. "Pip, we need your help. Tobias and Ian need your help," she pleaded. "Can you find us some clean wet towels and bandages?"

A warm, calming sensation ran into Pip as Valeen spoke. *We need your help,* she was saying, and his thoughts began to settle. *Bandages* . . . He looked at Tobias, and then at Valeen pressing the soaked towel against Tobias's neck, and snapped back into the moment. "Yes, we have a kit. It's in dry storage."

Valeen exhaled, deeply relieved she had Pip back. "Can you get it and bring it back here?" Laura's sobs captured their attention, and they looked across the room. A tarry dread sunk in Valeen's belly. "Pip, get the kit, and hurry."

Pip looked down at Tobias again. "I'll stay with him," Valeen reassured. "Hurry." Pip nodded and ran out of the room.

Valeen looked down at Tobias, pulling back the towel to inspect the cut. The bleeding seemed to be stopping, but he still looked pale and weak.

"It makes no sense," Tobias mumbled again.

"What, Tobias? What makes no sense?" Valeen pleaded. "Tobias, what happened?"

"I don't understand," Tobias replied in that same distant tone. He tried to shake his head and winced. The sharp pinch of pain seemed to temporarily bring him out of his stupor, and he instinctively reached for the source of pain, grabbing on to Valeen's hand again.

Valeen moved in front of him to be face to face, keeping one hand holding the blood-soaked towel in place, even though she didn't like turning her back to where Luke was. "Tobias, what happened?" she asked him again, periodically looking over her shoulder. She laid her other hand to rest on his leg and could feel the searing heat pulse through her and into Tobias, and then felt it move out and around them all. She was too distracted to think about the source right now she just knew with certainty it was not coming from only her. She was but a tool for some unseen power. Another thing to file away.

"Are they okay?" Tobias asked with sudden clarity, looking past Valeen's shoulder.

Valeen turned to look and saw Luke consoling Laura with his hand on her shoulder; he was saying something to her, speaking too softly for Valeen to hear. She had to get over there, but she told Pip she would stay with Tobias and didn't really want to leave Tobias unattended anyway.

Tobias swooned, validating her concerns. She quickly maneuvered to his side just as he fell heavily against her chest. She wrapped her arms around his body, cradling him in her lap with her chin resting atop his head. She looked across the room just as Luke looked up, making eye contact with her. His eyes burned with rage, and his expression was grim.

Valeen squeezed Tobias tightly. Closing her eyes, she let silent tears fall, releasing all the awfulness of the scene that had erupted around her.

***

Cornelius stumbled through the brush, tripping on rocks and fallen branches, desperately searching for a place to hide. Each faltered step caused agony to burn through his leg. He tripped and fell again, and this time he stayed down. He rolled onto his back and spotted a large bush about three yards away. Not risking standing again, he dragged himself to lie beneath it. Out of breath, he fell onto his back. His knee throbbed, making it hard to move around, and his head pounded, making it hard to concentrate.

He stared up at the soft lavender sky through empty patches of the bush. *There's something wrong with the sky. It should be nighttime.* His thoughts began to twist and turn as panic began to settle in. *I'm trapped, I cannot leave, the gateway is closed. There must be another gate, they can't all be closed. I never looked.* Cornelius dug deeply into his memories, searching for something he'd heard, something someone had said about any other gateways—but all he could see was Heather on that terrible day. She was so hurt and so angry. Her scream as she fell echoed through his whole body. *It was the dragons! The dragons blocked the way out.*

"No, no, no, that's not right," he whispered, then froze, his eyes darting, searching as far around him as he could without moving to make sure there was no one around who could have heard him. *The dragons cannot close the gateways. Only the Time Keepers can close the gateways. Did the dragons get to the Time Keepers and cast their sinister spells? Like they did with Tobias—they murdered him and made him a ghost!*

Again he searched, this time daring to move his head slightly, looking for any sign of the dragons or the ghosts that might have followed him. But there was nothing, no movement, no other sound, only stillness and silence . . . and something else. A calming energy began to take hold, and even though his whole body ached, it felt like the ground itself was pulling the pain and anguish right out of him.

Tobias was bleeding. He looked confused. Cornelius looked at the sharpened letter opener gripped in his hand and scowled. *Ghosts don't bleed. Where are all the dragons? The dragons are gone. Ghosts don't bleed . . .*

Splinters of memory flashed behind his eyes. *They were all bleeding and lying on the floor.* He looked at the blade in his hand again, and a flicker of dread bubbled in his stomach. *What have I done? The dragons are gone.* His thoughts were scrambled. He fought desperately for rationalization and clarity as his mind and body began to fade with exhaustion.

The dragons are gone . . . ghosts don't bleed . . . Those were his last thoughts before he lost consciousness.

***

Luke had his hand resting on Laura's shoulder, filling her with a calming spell, similar to what Valeen had done to Pip but more like the one he would cast on Sean, his young friend from his own realm. "Laura, can you hear me? Laura? He's not gone, he's only passed out."

Laura looked up at him, looking a little more than disheveled. Her eyes were red-rimmed and her sight blurry from tears. It felt like her heart and mind had fractured into a dozen pieces.

"Hear me, Laura," Luke said again, waiting until he saw her mind clear and had her attention. "He's alive. He is unconscious." Laura sobbed with relief, and Luke hastily grabbed a tablecloth from a fallen table and applied it to Ian's chest. "He'll be okay," he told Laura, taking both of her hands and putting them on top of the cloth. "Here, keep pressure on this. I'm going to go check on Val and Tobias, okay?"

Laura could only nod her agreement. She dared not speak, fearing she might come completely undone if she tried. Her very soul felt strangled by the reality of what she had just experienced.

Luke wiped absently at the blood on his mouth with the back of his wrist and stood up. The room spun, and his head felt like his brain was just swished in circles. He immediately bent, putting his hands on his knees until the dizziness passed. He gently touched the back of his head, where a good-sized lump was developing, and began to slowly stand again. This time, a thousand tiny piranhas bit into his back. Swearing under his breath, he made his way across the room to Valeen and Tobias.

Valeen visibly tensed even more when she saw Luke coming across the room, his expression gloomy and his body moving deliberately. She braced herself for the news.

Luke knelt slowly beside Valeen and Tobias, trying to avoid any further pinching pain in his back, wincing when he wasn't as successful as he'd hoped. He met Valeen's eyes and cupped her face with one hand. "You okay?"

"Ian?" was all she could say before she broke into sobs.

"Ian is okay. He'll have some recovering to do, but he's okay. How is he?" Luke gestured to Tobias.

Valeen just stared at Luke. It took a few minutes for her mind to catch up to what he was saying. Her first thought was to slug him, but she just didn't have the energy, so instead she took a deep breath. "I don't think anything too vital was cut; otherwise, I don't think he'd still be here. But he's still in pretty bad shape as far as I can tell. I think he still lost a lot of blood and is in shock."

Luke stood, cursing as he did, and made his way to one of the bedrooms. He yanked blankets off the bed, stopping to give one to Laura to put over Ian, pecking a kiss atop her head as he left her and brought the other to Tobias. "Cover him with this, keep him warm," he told Valeen.

"What the hell happened to your back?" Valeen asked, surprised when she saw the back of Luke's blood-soaked shirt.

"Glass, I think," he said, and glanced around the room, exhaling deeply. "Yeah, we're a mess."

"Pip went to find some medical supplies," Valeen told him, and, as if on cue, Pip stumbled through the door, dropping a large duffel bag and scattering some of its contents onto the floor. Luke moved quickly, catching Pip before he too hit the floor—growling at the pain in his back as he did, but another injured person was the last thing they needed.

"Are you okay?" Luke asked him.

"Yeah, I'm okay." Sweat-soaked strands of hair were pasted to his forehead, and he was breathing hard. "The General . . . he kept this . . . during the battle. I had to . . . dig it out," he said between breaths.

Luke patted him on the shoulder. "You did well, Pip," he told him. "I'm going to need you to be my assistant. Are you up for that?"

Pip's chest swelled with pride. "Yes, sir."

"Can you bring some wet towels and water to drink?" Luke asked as he unceremoniously dumped the rest of the supplies from the bag and began to gather up what he needed.

"Yes, sir," Pip replied with conviction, and ran out of the room yet again.

***

Valeen, Luke, and Laura had moved Tobias and Ian back down to the library. Pip had brought in blankets and pillows and kept everyone hydrated, running back and forth from the kitchen with pots of hot sterilized water and clean towels while Valeen, Luke, and Laura cleaned and mended wounds. Valeen was now straddled behind Luke on a chair, plucking pieces of glass out of his back with tweezers. Ian was lying on the couch, holding an ice pack against his jaw, his legs sprawled across Laura's lap. Tobias sat in another chair, staring distantly back to the scene of his father's rooms.

"I can't believe I passed out. What kind of man am I?" Ian asked rhetorically.

"The kind that took a blow to the face from an adrenaline-powered, trained soldier. I'm actually surprised you stayed standing as long as you did," Luke answered anyway. "Ouch! What are you doing back there, woman?"

"Stop being a baby," Valeen told him, focused on her task. "It was the last piece that I can see, but there might be some slivers that will have to make their way out on their own. None of them were very deep." She reached for the bottle of salve that was half empty now. It was some kind of ancient remedy made up of herbs and oils by some ancient realm; according to Luke and Pip, it was supposed to have miraculous healing power. Luke sighed with deep gratitude when she began to slather it over his back and its cooling medicine absorbed into his skin, bringing immediate relief to the tiny cuts.

"What happened, Tobias?" Laura, who had been quiet and dazed up until now, suddenly asked.

Tobias was barely listening to them as he pondered the insanity of what had happened. "I really don't know—it all happened so fast. One minute I was at the door, the next I was on the floor." He sat up and sighed deeply, staring down at his feet as he tried to put the random thoughts in order. The memories circled in his head while he tried to make sense of it all himself before he told the story.

Who are you? What have you done with my son? Cornelius had raged. He had tried to tell his father who he was, pleaded with him to understand. *No, you lie! The dragons demonized you! They murdered my son! I saw, I saw the fire! They cast an evil spell! They sent you to murder me like they murdered my sweet Heather!* Tobias searched for some kind of understanding in his father's expression, but there was no rational or reasonable thought behind the icy blue eyes that were brimming with tears and staring back at him. There was only an unrecognizable brink of madness.

Tobias had tried to explain that the dragons didn't cast spells (at least as far as he knew) and that his mother had fallen, that it was just an accident. The latter statement had surprised him. The absolute clarity of that truth made him feel strong, and he had tried to shove Cornelius away, feeling the blade cut into his neck as he did. That too was just an accident. Then he saw something break in his father as he lunged, tackling Tobias into a table, knocking him senseless. They had wrestled across the floor, and the next thing Tobias knew, Cornelius was on top of him, ready to plunge the blade into his chest, when Luke and Ian came busting through the door.

"Thank you for that, by the way," he told them, finishing the story.

For a moment, everyone was silent as the events unfolded in their own thoughts and they came to terms with their own emotions.

"I think we all feel like we lost a bar fight," Ian said, trying to lighten the mood.

"You did," Laura told him humorlessly, turning her sights on Tobias. "So, your father has gone off the deep end, then, right?" she said blatantly.

"Laura!" Ian scolded in a hushed voice.

"What? I'm just stating the facts. I was there, and I saw a madman attack and take down two grown men in a matter of minutes. And I was more scared than I have ever been. I thought I lost my husband and witnessed the murder of a young man." Laura waved her hand in the air as tears began to spill down her face. "Dragons! What were we thinking? This isn't some kind of petting zoo. This isn't the kind of vacation I had imagined. This has been terrifying." She hastily swiped at her tears. Angry with herself for losing control but not willing to apologize just yet, she went silent and turned her head away from them all.

Tobias hung his head in shame, not knowing how to comfort Laura or what words he could say to help her feel better. She was right; his father had 'gone off the deep end.' *Assuming that meant he went crazy.* Something went hot in his chest, and he couldn't hold it back. "It wasn't the dragons that did this," he told all of them, more aggressively than he intended. The embarrassment circled back around to shame, and he too looked away.

Valeen understood Laura's outburst and Tobias's. She didn't fault either of them for it. She knew all too well how everything could sometimes just explode out of you, and she felt a little guilty herself for bringing Laura here. It was a lot for Valeen to grasp at times, and she'd been living in strangeness her entire life. She also knew Laura would recover and feel bad and embarrassed, so for now she would just let her friend be where she was.

She looked over to Tobias and her heart broke. The boy was completely undone. "Tobias, I'm really sorry . . . I mean about your dad. No matter what he's done, it still has to be hard," she told him sincerely. She couldn't even imagine what he was feeling.

Tobias could only shrug a shoulder and glanced at Laura, who was still staring in the other direction. He didn't really know how he felt about his father, the dragons, or anything else.

Luke noticed Pip tightly holding his knees against his chest, leaning up against the wall, listening and watching intently as the intensity of the emotions circled the room. "We should all try to get some rest. It's been a long day—and night," he announced. "Ian, do you think you can make it back to your room?"

"I can if you can," Ian said. Swinging his legs off Laura's lap, he tentatively began to sit up. He leaned over and took Laura's hand, kissing her softly and painfully on the temple. "I'm okay, babe, we're all okay. And when we get home, I'll take you to a warm sandy beach somewhere."

Laura had her hand resting on her chin. Without looking at Ian, she smiled reluctantly. "You bet your ass you will." The statement eased some of the tension in the room.

Ian slowly stood up, groaning a bit as he did, and glanced down at Pip. "You okay, buddy?" he asked.

Laura just now realized Pip had been there the whole time, and a pang of guilt hit her heart. "You're welcome to stay on the couch in our rooms if you'd like," she told him.

Pip stood up, squaring his shoulders. "No, I'll be okay. Thank you."

Laura recognized the bravado for what it was. "Okay, will you help me get Ian up to bed and let me walk you to your room?"

Pip thought about it for a moment. He didn't want to be a scared baby, but the idea of Laura walking him to his rooms did comfort him a bit. He shrugged, feigning his courage. "Sure, you can if you want. Tobias, do you need help?" he asked, remembering Tobias was also injured.

Tobias grinned and touched his bandaged neck. "No, I think I'll be okay. You go ahead and get some rest. I'll see you in the morning."

Ian let Pip hold him steady around the waist, his arm draped over Pip's shoulder, even though he didn't really need any assistance. His legs were just fine. Laura followed them, carrying the blankets and pillow Ian had been using. Valeen and Luke were not far behind them.

"Tobias," Valeen called out, stopping him in the kitchen doorway to turn and look at her. "It will all work out," she told him.

He smiled halfheartedly. "Good night, Miss Valeen," he said, waving his arm behind him as he went through the door.

CHAPTER *Fifteen*

The dragons had found an abandoned cave where they brought in dry leaves and fallen branches to make a comfortable place to nest for the night. The hatchlings and younger dragons were cuddled beneath and against Mara's wings, feeling completely safe and peaceful for the first time in their young lives.

Lixten felt a wave of unease come over him and ruffled his wings restlessly. He glanced at Areve to see if she felt it also. In their unspoken language, Areve answered, *Yes, I felt it, but no souls have left the realm. I believe they are all all right.*

Areve heard Mara in her mind. She also had become restless and started to stand, causing the hatchlings to tumble from under her, grumbling and grunting as they scrambled to get back to the soft warmth of her body.

Tobias is safe, Mara. I don't know what happened, but they are safe and alive. You can feel that, can't you, Mara? Areve thought to her.

Mara quieted her mind and heart. She still had her reservations, but nodded her acceptance and settled back down, careful not to sit on any of the hatchlings, then leaned down to nudge one in the butt that was groggily scrambling to climb over and up onto the others.

The Time Keepers haven't opened the gateways yet. Why are they keeping them here? Lixten asked.

There are things to be mended and resolved, Areve answered cryptically. *We will return to the compound when it is time. The others are on their way, and we should meet up with them when the yellow sun is high. Let us rest now; there is work to be done.*

***

Before Pip went to bed, he had shown Laura how to secure the house, like he had done every night since he could remember, except this time it wasn't to keep out the dragons. She had walked him to his rooms but had not lingered, giving him some privacy and dignity. Pip vaguely remembered her coming back in the middle of the night to check on him, gently tucking the covers around him, kissing him softly on the head before tiptoeing out again.

He now stared out the kitchen window, waiting for the water to boil for the refined wheat he was preparing just for Ian. It would be warm and filling and easy for him to eat with his injured jaw.

He wasn't sure how he felt about Cornelius and what had happened. The General had taken care of him, given him a safe place to live. Although there was never any affection or real concern or interaction, Pip had been grateful for the comforts of shelter and warm meals. He had become content with being alone with his drawings and chores when Tobias had become so distant.

But all that had changed now. Everything was different. Tobias was his brother again, and the others, they were all so kind and caring, especially Laura and Ian. He really liked Ian. He liked the way he was genuinely interested in him, really listened to what he had to say. And Laura—she smelled so good; he felt safe and protected when she would hold on to him. His heart swelled at the thought of them, then disappointment dropped like stones in his belly. *They'll be leaving soon, when the gateways are open again.*

He buried the emotion, didn't want to think about it. *After all, I still have Tobias . . . and the dragons.* He felt a little ashamed now, after all these years of being so afraid of them, so afraid to go outside.

He peered out the window as he began to stir the wheat into the boiling water. He watched as the yellow sun cast its light across the compound, chasing the shadows up the buildings. He'd heard about this place having two suns, but he had never seen them before, at least not that he could remember. The more distant sun was blue, and the reason it was supposed to never be completely dark at night. But he couldn't recall a night that wasn't terrifyingly black.

He thought about going out and seeing the suns rise, feeling the warmth on his face and really looking around. He could also go in the evening, see what it looked like to see the suns set. *What would the colors be like?* he wondered. *Maybe the way this place was before the battle is in one of my drawings.* He'd have look through them after breakfast, but for now, he was thoroughly enjoying looking out the window at all the greens and multiple colors exploding into life right before his eyes. He shook his head, feeling embarrassed at his own silliness, but still he allowed a bit of giddiness to surface. *I can go outside! There is nothing to be afraid of.* A thrill of anticipation wriggled up his spine, and he eagerly picked up the pace to finish breakfast and go exploring. *Not too far, though,* he thought.

Ian ambled into the kitchen just as he was setting out bowls. "I made you some hot cereal," Pip said. "I thought it might be easier for you to eat. Oh, and I made coffee. I think I did it right."

Ian reached for a cup and scowled at the sore tightness across his chest. "I'm sure you did just fine, Pip," he said through semi-gritted teeth. His jaw wasn't broken, but it hurt like hell when he tried to talk. *It's just a little morning stiffness, nothing Valeen can't assist with,* he told himself, keeping the frustration and anger at bay. He still didn't really understand how it all worked, even after everything he had witnessed in the last year and had now experienced with the dragons. *That was cool.* He was open and believed, but he hadn't really been a part of it before. *It was pretty amazing.*

"Thank you for all this, Pip, but you know, you don't have to wait on us," Ian told him with his back turned while he filled his cup. "We all actually enjoy your company and like having you around. You don't have to be doing something for us just to hang out."

When he turned around, Pip was scowling. His expression was both confusion and delight. "But I like doing things for you," he finally said.

Ian grinned and ruffled his hair. "Fair enough," he told him, taking a sip of his coffee. "Mm-hmm, this *is* good, Pip, you did do well. Thank you."

Pip beamed a proud smile at him and continued setting the table with a little perk in his step.

***

Ian and Pip worked together on breakfast. It was becoming a morning routine, one that Pip would sorely miss when Ian went back to his own realm, but for now he would enjoy the time they had together. Tobias and Luke sauntered in, looking and feeling much like Ian: beat-up and sore, their muscles stiff, resisting movement.

Ian reached for a cup and handed it to Luke. "So where are our beautiful ladies?" he asked.

Luke took the cup with overwhelming gratitude and poured himself some coffee, softly blowing and taking a sip before answering. "They're still getting themselves together. They'll be down shortly, I imagine."

Ian nodded his understanding and joined Tobias, Luke, and Pip at the table, letting the ham cook on its own. "How you holding up?" he asked Tobias.

Tobias ran his hands through his hair, then gingerly touched the bandage on his neck. "I'm okay. It doesn't hurt very much anymore."

Ian stared at Tobias from across the table until Tobias looked up at him. "That's not what I meant. How are you holding up?" he asked again, the meaning evident in his tone.

Tobias exhaled and slumped in his chair. "I really haven't decided yet. None of this makes any sense. I thought I knew who he was." He took another deep breath. "I thought I knew who I was, who the dragons were. There was an order in the chaos. I had a purpose. Now I feel like I don't know anything." He went silent, gathering his thoughts. Luke, Ian, and Pip quietly waited for him to continue.

"I was thinking as I got dressed this morning, I usually go over what my chores are for the day. Taking care of the dragons is what I did—avoiding my father, harboring the resentment, and holding on to the bitterness of the injustices while I'm blindly doing the General's bidding. And now . . . now I feel this guilt . . . I could have done something. I could have paid more attention. All these years I just did what I was told, never asked any questions. I thought I was helping the dragons, thought I was doing something good, when in reality I was keeping them prisoners as much as my father." He rubbed the heels of hands into his eyes. "Gods, my father. What can I do? I'm so mixed up. I saw something in him last night. Something I had never recognized before, never looked for. He was afraid. He's always been afraid. And all the bitterness and resentment turned to something else . . . and I can't really identify it."

He sat up in his chair, leaning his elbows on the table, and looked around at the stunned faces of the men and young boy staring back at him. He barked out a laugh. "Sorry about that. I guess I've never really gotten honest with or really looked at what was going on inside my own head. Maybe the dragons did cast some kind of spell." He chuckled.

Luke and Ian took a sip of their coffee simultaneously, looking over the rims to study Tobias. Pip, not knowing what to say or do either, followed suit, sipping on his hot chocolate, leaving a foamy mustache over his lip.

"I don't believe it's ever too late to discover who and what's inside you," Luke told Tobias, thinking of Valeen's journey.

"So what's next?" Ian asked, wanting to move the conversation on, allowing Tobias to process what he was just starting to feel.

Luke shrugged. "I really have no idea. I haven't felt a shift in the gateways, and I don't know why we still have to be here. Have either of you heard or felt anything from Lixten or Areve?" he asked Tobias and

Ian.

"No, I haven't," Ian said. "But I'm not sure I'd recognize it if I did. I've been . . . a little distracted." He gently rubbed his bruised jaw.

"Right. Tobias, what about you?" Luke asked. But Tobias was staring at something distant in his mind. "Tobias, are you all right?" he asked, a little concerned, taking into account Tobias's recent outburst.

"Yeah, I think so," Tobias responded with a distant tone. "I just don't have anything to do."

Ian gingerly patted his chest and got up to turn the ham frying on the stove. "Well, there are the horses that need to be attended to. I'd be willing to give you a hand if you'd like."

"Can I help?" Pip asked excitedly before Tobias could answer.

Tobias took a deep breath and stood up to assist Ian, ruffling Pip's hair as he passed. "I don't see why not," he told Pip, with as much delight for Pip's excitement as the boy had.

Luke sat back again, holding his cup against his chest. "Maybe while we're here we can clean up a bit outside. You know, like dismantle the doors to the buildings, maybe turning them into piles of rubble. Do you have any dynamite lying around, Tobias?" he asked, only half kidding.

Tobias began breaking eggs into a large bowl. "Hah! If I were Areve, I'd just burn the whole compound to the ground." The thought of Areve's fire pinched something in his belly. Lixten and Mara had no fire, and he blamed himself.

Pip went quiet, lowering his head and staring into his cup. "But where would we live?" he blurted out, not realizing the men weren't completely serious. He raised his head, glancing at all of them while searching for his courage. "What about the General?" he mumbled.

The three men stopped what they were doing, feeling a little ashamed at their comments, and looked at each other. Tobias turned and stared out the window. "He's right. We can't just leave him out there."

Luke stood and also moved to stare out the window. "Yeah, you're right, we can't. But it's obvious the man is dangerous," he said, instantly regretting his choice of words. He didn't want to insult Tobias.

Tobias felt Luke's unease. "It's all right, Luke. He is dangerous, and not just to us."

***

Valeen came out of her room to find Laura staring out the barred window. Without saying anything, Valeen went to stand next to her. "It is really quite beautiful, isn't it?" Laura said, not turning away from the view.

Valeen's breath hitched in her throat when she gazed out the window and, like Laura, couldn't look away. It was like they'd woken up in a different place entirely. Had they traveled in their sleep to some kind of majestic land? The once-barren trees were now lush and dense with different shades of green and indigo leaves. The bushes and shrubs were thick and thriving with bursts of rust-colored berries scattered through them. Red-leaved vines with bright yellow flowers crept up the side of the buildings that were even more like ancient, weathered ruins. She also noticed fluttering and buzzing movements here and there throughout the compound. And over it all was a silvery, shimmering glow cast from the rays of the shining sun just beginning its ascent. It was breathtaking. *This is what Luke wanted to share with us*, she thought, and her heart sank at the thought of the disappointment he must have felt. She understood why he'd been so determined to find out what happened, and how torturous it would have been for Tobias and Pip to watch all this die and fade away to become what it was by the time they'd first arrived.

"What happened, Val?" Laura asked, still peering out the window in awe.

"I have no idea, but it can't be a bad thing, right?" Valeen replied, also still unable to look away from the scenery.

Laura turned to face her, leaning against the windowsill and crossing her arms over her chest. "How do you do it, Val?"

"Do what?" Valeen answered, still looking out the window in wonderment.

"How can you go from the terrifying experience just last night to, well, this?" Laura said, gesturing toward the view outside. "To see such amazing beauty that literally brings your soul to the surface of your being in just a matter of hours. How do you stay sane?"

Valeen reluctantly turned away from the window and looked down at her shoes. "I don't know that I do. As a matter of fact, there have been several occasions I thought about committing myself into a mental hospital, and it wasn't even that long ago." She thought about it for a minute, asking herself the same question. "I guess it's about learning to stay in the moment I'm in, which is not as easy as you'd think."

"Hah!" Laura barked out.

"I know, right? I guess it's just one of those things you don't realize you can achieve until you've actually done it. I suppose the more you become aware and accept that there is so much going on around us all the time—we were just oblivious to it—the easier it becomes to just go with it."

Laura glanced sideways at Valeen. "You are crazy. You know that, right?"

Valeen chuckled. "Yeah, I know. Come on, I'm hungry and in desperate need of some coffee," she said, tugging on Laura's sleeve. They both turned for one last look at the spectacular view out the window and headed down to meet up with their men.

"You're just in time," Ian said as they came into the kitchen. "We have eggs, hot cereal, and ham. Apparently all the meat we have is ham. Ruben?" he questioned, looking at Pip, who nodded cheerfully, pleased that Ian had paid attention. "Well, Ruben, the cook, went for more supplies that would have included bacon and sausage, but, well, he hasn't quite made it back yet." Ian set the plate of warm ham on the table and moved to Laura, taking her by the hands. "Are you okay?" he asked, searching her face for any sign of distress.

"I'm okay. Really, I am," she reassured. "One minute at a time, right, Val?"

"Yep," Valeen answered, moving purposefully to the coffee pot. Reaching for a cup from the cupboard, she looked out the window. "Have you guys seen outside yet?" she asked, still in awe of the view.

Luke came up behind her, wrapping his arms around her waist and pecking a kiss on the side of her head. "We have. We were just talking about going out to start clearing things away and taking care of the horses," he told her, also peering out the window.

"Is this the way you remembered it from when you were a boy?" Valeen asked him.

"Almost," Luke replied. "The difference is the trees and skies were full of dragons."

"There will be again," Tobias added with conviction.

Luke spun Valeen around to face him, grinning widely. "You hungry?" he asked.

"I'm famished," Valeen said, playfully pushing past him with her coffee in hand, taking a seat at the table with the others. When everyone was settled and had their plates full in front of them, she looked at Tobias. "Luke and I were talking about how you and Ian were able to hear and understand Areve and the other dragons, before we were . . . interrupted."

138

Tobias took a bite of his food, allowing himself to think about how to answer. The truth was he'd really never thought about it. It was something he'd always done. As he looked around at the eager faces around the table waiting for an explanation, his thoughts reeled. Thank the gods Luke took over.

"I was telling her it was like a different frequency," Luke began. "All beings have a language of their own. The Time Keepers have their own. The fairies have their own. And we have our own. Some can speak several languages—like, back home, some people know French or Hungarian. Some can speak both, and some can only speak one, but all have a tone and a vibration to them. You can know what is happening without knowing exactly what they're saying." He turned to look at Valeen. "Do you remember that couple that came into Ella's a few weeks ago? Even though we didn't understand what they were saying to each other, we knew the woman was upset and the man was trying to console her simply by their tones and body language."

"I get that," Valeen said. "But I don't think that is the same as, well, this." She gestured to Ian and Tobias. "This is different, their reading the minds of the dragons." She put her hand on her forehead. "That still sounds so strange to me."

"Me too," Laura added, pushing her plate away. "This whole experience is strange." The weariness in her was apparent. "One minute at a time," she mumbled to herself, breathing deeply. Valeen made eye contact with her friend and smiled reassuringly at her.

Ian also pushed his plate away. "I don't think it's that strange when you consider where we are. I mean, seriously, we're on Planet Dragon. The way I take care of my horses and know what they need or what they might be feeling is really not that different; it's just more intensified or more defined in this particular place, right?" he asked Luke.

Luke winced at the term "planet." "It's not a different planet, Ian. It's more of an extension of a reality," he said, a bit more hotly than he intended. "But yes, that's about right. It has a vibration and frequency of its own also." He turned back to Valeen. "I think it's like how you could speak to Mary when she was in the void. It was a language you could speak, an extension of reality . . ." He eyed Ian. ". . . you could enter into."

Valeen sat back in her chair. "Okay, so what about that bug, that dragonfly?" she asked, waving her arm in the air. "I've never been able to actually *hear* insects talk before."

"Yes, you have," Ian replied. "You just haven't heard them with your ears, but you still are able to feel their vibrations, and again, I believe the reason we can hear Sabastian so clearly is because of the different plan—" He quickly corrected himself. "—extension of reality we're in."

Tobias was listening intently to the conversation, getting the answers to questions he asked himself so often, but this one answer he knew absolutely. "Sabastian can communicate in all frequencies and vibrations. It is one of the things that make his kind so magical and powerful. He can most definitely be annoying at times, but in reality, dragonflies are revered as one of the most powerful beings in all the realms, coming in only second to the Time Keepers."

With unspoken acceptance, they moved the conversation to what they could do while they waited for further enlightenment, for some sign or instruction from the dragons or until the Time Keepers opened the gateways.

***

Sabastian found the dragon's lair by accident. It was the hatchlings frolicking in the bushes that got his attention, and he knew the adults would be keenly watching over them, even if he could not see them. *Happy, happy babies, yes, yes.* He searched the area for the lair; it would be close. Then he spotted it, camouflaged by thick green bushes and vines covering the top and opening.

He flew straight to the opening, only to bump right into Mara's snout as she emerged slowly through the hanging limbs. Her colors shimmered in the dappled sunlight that shone through the tall trees. Although the hit was like a running into a solid wall to Sabastian, it was but a tiny twinge on Mara's snout. *Oh, excuse me, Your Majesty,* Sabastian told her, but Mara only huffed at him through her nostrils, causing him to tumble backward. She offered him a passing glance, then turned her attention to the sky.

She opened her wings, flapping them slowly as if testing their strength and, in one quick movement, leapt into the trees, dodging, weaving, and maneuvering through the branches with incredible speed and grace until she broke through the tops. Sabastian felt exhausted and weary from his search, but as he watched her climb and circle the trees, brushing the tips with her belly, a surge of excitement rejuvenated him. He watched her circle and dive then climb again. She dove again, gaining velocity, then abruptly pulled up just above the tree line. Sabastian buzzed happily over the hatchlings as they followed her movements on the ground, tumbling and tripping over rocks, fallen branches, and each other, chirping with delight in the dance.

Mara slowed, coming to an abrupt stop in the air. Hovering, she shifted so her belly faced the rising sun. Its rays glinted off her lavender and indigo colors, lighting up golden flecks and swirls that Sabastian had not seen before. Her whole being seemed to glow in the light.

And then he heard it: a hum that vibrated through the air and trees like a hundred violins in perfect synchrony, the sound every stringed instrument in every realm had tried to mimic. Like the trees and foliage around him, his whole body quivered. It had been so long since he'd heard their music that he had almost forgotten how it moved right into your soul. It was the song of dragons. *They can hear! They can, Tobias can hear! The song of freedom, yes, yes. The General, he will hear . . . the General!* he remembered suddenly and flew back to the opening of the lair.

He found Areve and Lixten blissfully basking in Mara's song. They looked so peaceful he didn't want to disturb them. "Uh-hum. Um, Your Majesties?" he apologetically began. "I have some news."

Areve opened her eyes and looked warmly down at him. "What is it, Sabastian?" she asked, untroubled at the interruption.

"It's the General. He has gone mad, he has, yes." Sabastian hung his head. "Yes, yes, mad and so sad."

Lixten too opened his eyes. "What has happened, Sabastian?" he asked in alarm, recalling his uneasiness the night before.

Sabastian relayed the story in detail while Areve and Lixten listened intently, their compassion and shock evident in their lack of response.

"Is Tobias all right?" Mara asked from the entrance to the lair, her tone dripping with resentment and vengeance.

None of them had realized she'd returned. Sabastian startled at the sound of her voice, a little afraid of what she might do. She was known for irrational outbursts, and it was Tobias who was able to calm her down and put her at ease, but Sabastian felt confident in Areve's authority and answered anyway. "Yes, yes. Miss Valeen, she is healer. She heals, she does, she does."

"The General is out there somewhere, broken and unstable," Lixten began, with a hint of panic in his voice that made him feel ashamed.

Areve felt his discontent and moved to face him. "I agree he might be as irrational as a wounded animal, but he is only a threat to himself and his kind now. Your agreement has been dissolved. There is no more need to surrender our souls to the atrocities you and the others have endured. Senseless death is not our way," she told him, glancing over her shoulder to Mara to affirm she understood as well, and then back to Lixten. She moved closer to him, rubbing her head atop his, and spoke into his mind. *Lixten, there is nothing to warrant your shame. You stopped the killing, allowed the others to escape and live. Even I left to the Quiet Place—do you hold resentment for me?*

Lixten jerked back. "Of course not! You did what you had to; you stayed alive, you kept all of us alive."

"So did you," Areve told him firmly.

"Yes, yes, alive, we are all alive! Yes," Sabastian chattered excitedly while hopping up and down on Areve's back.

Lixten nodded reluctantly. Areve was right, but he still felt weak. He had no fire; he'd allowed it to be taken from him and from Mara, allowed them to be held captive and used as breeding tools for a madman. He just couldn't let go of the feeling he had let them all down, had brought shame to them all.

***

Valeen and the others were just finishing the cleanup and the putting away of breakfast when they felt the wave of energy wash over the compound. The windows rattled, and the hairs on their bodies stood up. Everyone went still and quiet. Then the sound came: It was like the hum of a string orchestra, similar to Areve's laughter, Valeen recalled. They all looked at each other. Then, all at once, they ran out the door into the compound.

"Is that the dragons?" Pip asked, not sure if he was feeling excited or terrified. The sound was scary, but at the same time it made him feel all warm inside.

"It's only one, and she's happy," Tobias said, resting a hand on Pip's shoulder as they both stared out into the trees.

"She?" Laura questioned.

"It's Mara," Ian answered.

"Mara? How do you know that?" Laura asked, a little irritated that he knew at all and not sure why it irritated her.

"I can feel her. She has her own voice," Ian replied, smiling.

Luke stood with his hands in his pockets, rocking back on his heels, a satisfied grin on his face. "She's singing," he said to no one in particular.

Valeen was only half listening to what everyone was saying around her. She stood with her head tilted up, closing her eyes and feeling the warmth of the sun on her face as she let the sound vibrate through her. It felt like her very every cell in her body ignited and shone out from her being. For a fleeting moment, she thought she heard voices echo in the back of her mind, and then they were gone.

As she slowly opened her eyes, it all became very clear. "I think I know what they want us to do."

CHAPTER *Sixteen*

The trembling ground and shivering branches awoke Cornelius. His head was pounding, and his whole body felt stiff and sore. Disoriented, he tried to place where he was. *What a horrible dream,* he thought while lying there trying to get his bearings.

A cool line slithered across his chest, and he absently went to brush it away. His hand caught on something, and when he looked, there was a small garter snake intertwined through his fingers. Shock and panic had him sitting up abruptly, unaware he was still under a bush and not in his bed. The sting from a branch cutting across his cheek made him jerk back, causing his leg to scream with pain, protesting against the movement. He struggled to maneuver from under the bush, snagging and tearing his clothes on the tiny thorns protruding on the branches as he scooted out.

When he was finally clear, he slumped on the ground, sweating and breathing hard through the agony until it subsided to a dull throb. He looked around at his surroundings in confused awe. There were blooming flowers and budding leaves. He heard the sound of birds chirping and . . . something else. His mind felt like it was being wrung out like a washcloth; his thoughts swirled. It felt like he was looking through the shards of a shattered mirror, fragmented pieces of memory that made no sense. He saw broken slivers of himself and Heather and Tobias—past, present, and a horrifying future all at once. Arriving here with an infant Tobias. Tobias pleading with him, then bleeding on the floor. Heather smiling at him, holding out her hand, then falling. Dragons setting the house aflame. Heather standing next to an enormous dragon, smiling again, falling, falling into blackness. He saw himself being flung through the air by sharp talons. Fire erupting. Men screaming and running. Tobias with Pip on the floor, staring accusingly. Voices. He heard the orders: "Go there, talk to them." He felt the fear clench in his belly. *I am a soldier.* "Take your family, take Heather." *I must follow my orders.* "Take them." They insisted he bring Heather and Tobias." *Why?* Heather was falling. Heather, she wanted to come, she was eager to come. *Why did she want to come to this place? I must follow orders.* Fear turned to terror. *They were bigger than I thought. They are dangerous. I have to protect my wife and son.* Heather reaching out to them, reaching for him. Pleading and crying . . . falling. Tobias bleeding. *They were ghosts. Ghosts don't bleed.*

His thoughts broke and spun and broke again. *What is that sound? Music?* He looked down, studying the dried blood that streaked his fingers and palms, his torn and bloody clothes. He tried desperately to put a solid thought together. *What has happened?* The music . . . it wasn't the thrumming in his head. It was coming from all around him. *It's in the trees and bushes; it's in the air.* The sound touched his mind and heart, soothing the chaos.

His emotions overflowed. He put his face in his bloodstained hands and began to sob. *What is happening? What is happening to me? The dragons, they are doing this . . .*

***

Areve was brought out of her blissful thoughts when dozens of voices, whispering and mumbling, exploded in her mind. *They're close, they are coming.*

With the agility and grace of a queen, she sprang to the entrance and pushed through the opening. She searched the skies, eager to greet the return of her family. Mara perched atop the entrance of their lair with the same excited anxiousness and, like Areve, searched the skies for the first glimpse of those who had waited for so long.

Then they saw it—a shadowed formation moving toward them. Areve's chest filled with joy and pride as the shadows began to transform into a dance of colors and light, separating into individual shapes and sizes. When she didn't think her heart could swell any more, she saw the movement in the trees and bushes under the flight. *There are more young ones,* she thought, and tears of delight swam in her eyes.

Lixten heard the voices in his own mind and sighed. What could he possibly say to them? They had lived in seclusion and fear for years because he'd given up; apologies just didn't seem like enough. *And now look at me, tattered and beat down. I don't have any fire. I mated not for love or care, but like an animal, following only instinct. All those beautiful souls were taken away and slain because of my actions. I am not a prince. I am a disgrace to my tribe.* He stood but couldn't move forward, couldn't bring himself to face them.

145

***

Ian and Tobias finished grooming and rubbing down the horses; they were just about to start mucking out the corrals. Tobias had a pitchfork in his hand and started to open one of the gates. The squeal of the hinges made both men stop what they were doing and look at each other. Tobias nodded at Ian's unspoken words. "Enough" was all he said, and they began to open all the gates to let the horses out. Most took the opportunity to run out the open doors into the trees. Only Rosy sauntered to the opening and chose to stay and graze just outside the doors.

"I guess she's staying," Ian said, and walked to an old workbench. After a moment of shuffling through rusted tools and stuck drawers, he found two screwdrivers. Smiling, he tossed one to Tobias, and without another word, they began taking the hinges off the gates.

Valeen and Luke seemed to have the same idea and took on the task of dismantling the doors to the concrete buildings. Using knives from the kitchen, they cut every line that operated the mechanical doors, including the one to the front door of the house.

While the others were busy outside, Laura and Pip went through the house, opening every door and window to let the air circulate the scent of flowers and fresh, clean air throughout. Laura made her way to Cornelius's rooms and stood in the threshold of the doorway. Broken glass, toppled furniture, and smeared patches of crimson on the floor made her feel sick to her stomach as the memories of the incident flashed before her eyes. She took a deep breath and stepped deliberately into the room. The crunch of debris under her feet almost had her running back out, but instead she gathered her courage and headed for the windows. *Of all the rooms, this one needs the fresh air the most,* she decided.

The first window she went to wouldn't budge. Frustrated tears welled in her eyes; she just wanted out of this room. Then, with one final heave, it opened, and she hastily moved to the other rooms where the windows opened more easily.

When she went to leave, she turned once more to the scene. Although the air gently blowing through was refreshing, the site still made her uneasy, and she decided to just close the door. She watched the room slowly disappear in sections as she pulled the door closed, and for a moment she just stood there gripping the knob. So many different emotions filled her all at once, and she couldn't stop the silent tears from falling.

Is this what Val goes through? Enduring so many up and down moments in a matter of days? It's a wonder she has any sanity left at all. And suddenly it all became very clear to her, and she understood. *This is what it's all about, the moving on, going forward for the good of all of it—for the good of the whole.* Her heart swelled. She had always loved Valeen. Valeen was a sister to her, but now she got it. She felt not only blessed but honored to be a part of Valeen's life, getting to experience these strange, sometimes scary adventures with her friend, and she realized she had a part in all of it. Valeen needed her as much as she needed Valeen. *We are one force, all of us: me, Ian, Luke, Val, Pip, the dragons. We are all one entity. Even Krista and Racine had a part to play.*

And in a matter of moments, the tears of confusion and uncertainty turned to tears of gratitude and sureness. She exhaled heavily and swiped the tears from her face, wiping the wetness on her jeans. When she turned to leave, she was startled by Pip, who was standing at the other end of the hall near the stairs, just watching her.

For a moment, neither of them spoke. As Laura looked at him, all she saw was this boy who had been witness to and survived unspeakable things. He was so young to have to go through what he had, but seeing him now, she became very aware of the human spirit, confirming what she'd just come to understand within herself. In a matter of days, this young boy had overcome a fear that had held him prisoner for most of his short life. Then, something seemed to unlock simultaneously in her heart and mind, something she would ponder later.

"I think we're all finished up here," she said cheerfully, walking toward Pip. "I don't know about you, but I'm getting hungry. Why don't we go find the others and take a break?" As she approached, she causally put her arm across his shoulders, turning him away from the direction of the room and leading him back down the stairs.

Pip shrugged under her hands. "Okay, I guess I'm kinda getting hungry too," he said, letting Laura guide him down the stairs in the safety of her arms.

Valeen and Luke were gathering up tools, pieces of hose, and other debris when a gust of wind blew through the compound. Valeen heard the horses whinny in the nearby trees, pulling her attention away from her task. They galloped in circles and pawed at the ground; they seemed more excited than frightened.

Instinctively shielding her eyes with her hand, Valeen looked into the sky. In the distance she could see a small, dark cloud moving toward them. Luke had gone to stand in the center of what was once a slushy, muddy road where now there were tiny blades of grass beginning their ascent. Tobias walked out of the stables and Ian followed, both searching the skies. Valeen walked over to stand next to Luke, laying her hand on his shoulders. "Is that the dragons?" she wondered.

"Yes," Luke answered with that same satisfied grin she had seen so often as he gazed out into the trees.

Laura and Pip were just approaching the door through the kitchen when they felt the wind blow over them. They listened to its subtle whistle, like an entity of its own, as it moved purposefully through the house, clearing out the residual unpleasantness of what lingered. Laura spotted Valeen and the others standing in the middle of the road. She and Pip glanced at each and, without a word, went to where everyone was standing.

"What is happening?" she asked Ian, coming up behind him.

Ian really couldn't answer her; he wasn't sure himself. He just knew he felt lighter all of a sudden, more so than he recognized as his usual cheerful, easygoing self. Laura followed his gaze and saw the dark formation in the sky. "What is that?"

"They're dragons," Valeen told her.

"Dragons?" Laura asked skeptically. "But I thought they would be bigger."

"They're still a few miles away," Luke told her, still captivated by the dance in the distant sky, where glints of light and color flashed as the formation moved and swayed like a flock of birds through the air.

"Miles?" Laura asked, realizing the enormity of what she was seeing. "Did they create that blast of wind?"

"I don't think so," Valeen said, also not looking away from the scene playing out in the distance.

"The Time Keepers have opened the gateways," Tobias answered absently.

"Opened the gateways?" Laura wondered yet again.

Valeen looked over to her friend. "Laura, really?" she said with humor.

"I know, I know, I sound like a dolt. Going with the flow is still new to me." Laura wrapped her arm around Pip and smiled down at him. "Well, I guess we just have to wait to see what happens next, right?"

Pip nodded and stepped a little closer to her. He liked the way she made him feel so safe.

"I didn't think there would be so many still alive," Tobias said in that same distant tone, indicating that he was still working it all out in his own mind. *Grundles,* he remembered Sabastian telling them.

They all watched as the cloud of dragons maneuvered and dived below the trees, then disappeared. Luke exhaled and turned to face Valeen. "Well, I guess we get to choose."

"Choose? Choose what?" Laura asked. When the others just looked at her, she smiled under the blush. "Sorry. Is anybody hungry?" she cheerfully asked, changing the subject.

Ian chuckled and wrapped his arms around both Pip and Laura, pecking a kiss on the side of Laura's head. "I love your brain. Let's eat."

"Yeah, I could eat," Luke told them, taking Valeen around the waist and guiding her toward the house. He glanced back at Tobias, who was still studying the empty sky. "Tobias, let's take a break, figure out our next move," he called back. Tobias nodded and reluctantly turned away to follow them in.

***

Areve and Mara waited in anxious anticipation as Praxton led dozens of dragons to land with graceful agility in the trees and on the ground. Some wore horrific scars of battle and torture, while others' expressions were of great regret and shame. It broke Areve's heart, but she greeted them with dignity and respect nonetheless. She noticed some of the females were releasing eggs from their talons, laying them gently at their feet as they all gathered around their queen's lair. Then the brush burst open as younger ones of various ages broke through. Areve's eyes filled with grateful tears, amazed at the numbers that had survived.

Praxton approached her with pride and bowed. "Your Majesty, I have brought your family home as you bid."

Areve scowled down at him and, using her snout, lifted his head to look at her. "You do not do my bidding, Praxton," she told him sternly. Then she looked up and around at the others. *None of you do my bidding. I do not rule you. You rule yourselves, as is evident in your survival. We have been given new information from the other realms, and we must abide by our wisdom. There are humans in the realm that have chosen to assist in healing our land and our souls.* She shifted her thoughts to focus on Lixten only.

149

Lixten heard the rustling of trees and bushes, the chirps and happy squawks of the young, and to his surprise, he felt his heart warm as he listened to Areve greet the others. Then he heard her thoughts shift to him. *You must come out. You will see.*

Lixten tentatively pushed his way through the opening of the lair, ready to take the assault that he deserved, but as he emerged, he saw the many faces of his family bearing the memories of battle wounds and defeat that now held hope. And then he spotted Praxton, his and Ari's son. His sleekness resembled his mother, and Lixten knew immediately that he also had her gift of night vision, but his colors were Lixten's own. Pride swelled in his chest, and overwhelming gratitude for Tobias, who'd so diligently and lovingly looked after his son. He approached Praxton with deliberate focus.

Lixten's advance made Praxton nervous. He looked around at the others for reassurances. He didn't know what to expect; Lixten was three times his size in height and girth. When Areve smiled warmly at him, he relaxed a bit and looked up at Lixten uncertainly. Lixten just stared down at him and, in a flash of movement, intertwined his neck with Praxton's.

As Lixten slowly let go, he stared out at the faces surrounding him, searching for hostility and reproach from them, but what he saw instead made his blood surge. Among the faces, he recognized the females he'd been forced to mate with, alive and coddling the hatchlings that Tobias had released. *They're alive! How? Why? The General took them away. I never saw them again.* He felt no resentment, no anger. He only felt and heard in his mind the relief and respect that emitted from his family.

His thoughts were interrupted by the sound of breaking branches and grumbling, followed by the thud and grunt of someone hitting the ground. Areve was shocked when she saw the human stumble out of the bushes, brushing away debris from his torn and dirty clothes, grinning like a madman. Even more disconcerting was that her alarm didn't ripple through the tribe of dragons as she expected.

***

Valeen and the others sat around the table, empty plates and half-full drinks in front of them.

"I realize that I keep asking what might be considered mundane questions, but what is it we get to choose?" Laura asked the room. "Not that this hasn't been a fun adventure," she continued sarcastically, immediately regretting the statement. Groaning, she rubbed her hands over her face and dropped them on table. "I apologize. I'm tired and punchy, and a little homesick."

Pip was sitting between Ian and Laura, and in her frustration, Laura didn't notice him drop his head and sigh, but Ian did. He playfully rubbed the top of Pip's head, mussing up his hair and smiling down at him, letting him know it would all be okay. Pip looked up at Ian, halfheartedly grinning back, unconvinced it would be.

Luke leaned forward, clasping his hands on the table, contemplating the words he wanted to say. "The Time Keepers have opened the gateways, and I know we're all ready to go home. But what if we have an opportunity here? Cornelius is still out there, and I'm pretty sure he doesn't know the gateways are open. I'm not sure he knows much of anything right now." He paused for a moment, searching the faces of those seated around him. When no one said anything, he continued. "I'm just saying I think we all need to see this through. To me, it doesn't feel like we're finished, but I think we get to choose what to do next. Unfortunately, I'm not sure what exactly that is." He glanced at Valeen and waited for someone to respond.

"I think I can heal the fire," Valeen blurted out. "But I think I'll need help. It feels like it's a bit more than just healing another human being's wounds."

Laura stood up abruptly. "Okay, let's do this," she said with anxious conviction, ending any chance of further debate. "Ian, can I talk to you alone for a moment?" she asked cryptically.

"Um, sure," Ian said, looking around the room at the baffled expressions, searching for some kind of assurance that nobody would let him be killed. When no one answered his unspoken plea, he scooted away from the table. "Okay, how about we take a walk outside? Keep the witnesses to a minimum," he told Laura—jokingly, he hoped.

Valeen and Luke chuckled as Laura led Ian out the door. "I guess that settles it, then," Luke told them. Tobias smirked, but he hadn't really been paying attention. He had been devising a plan. He knew what he had to do, and it was breaking his heart.

Pip stayed solemn and quiet. "May I be excused?" he mumbled.

Tobias jerked at the meekness in his tone. He'd thought Pip had gotten past all that. "You don't have to ask, Pip. If you're done, you can leave the table," he told him, more harshly than he intended. Pip didn't reply; he just hastily got up and hurried down to his rooms. "Oh hells,"

Tobias said, rubbing his hand over face. "I should go talk to him."

Luke took Valeen by the hand, squeezing gently. "He'll be okay. I think he might need to be alone for a while. Give him some time."

Valeen reached across the table to take Tobias's hand. "It has been an . . . intense week. It's been a lot for us, let alone a young boy. He has already shown incredible courage, but even young boys need to have time to sort it all out."

Tobias sighed. "Yeah, you're right. *I* still haven't sorted it all out. What am I supposed to do about my father?" he asked abruptly, catching Luke and Valeen off guard. They both blinked in surprise at the suddenness of the question.

Tobias stood and started clearing the table. "I don't think he's a threat to the dragons anymore . . ." He stopped moving, holding a plate in each hand. "So many . . . I didn't realize," he mumbled to himself, shaking his head in disbelief and continuing his task. "But I really don't think I want him killed either." He set the plates in the sink and turned to face Luke and Valeen, leaning against the edge. "I don't believe they would go hunting for him, but if he threatened them, they might react. That could end badly for him."

Valeen and Luke just stared at Tobias. He appeared to be more . . . mature, for lack of a better word—clear and focused. It amazed Valeen as she thought about how, in just a short few days, the people she'd met when they first arrived had transformed right in front of her eyes. Even Laura seemed . . . different.

Luke cleared his throat, sat back heavily in his chair, and glanced at her. "Well, I guess we should go find him, then. We can round up and saddle a couple of the horses."

Tobias just nodded. He had gone back into his thoughts. "So many," he said again, shaking his head and turning back to the sink to stare out the window.

"He needs help, Tobias. Not to be imprisoned or killed—just help," Valeen told him compassionately.

"Yeah," Tobias sighed. "I just know if he's aware of that, and that's what scares me. My father can be . . . difficult, even when he's . . . himself. I can't imagine what he's feeling or thinking at this point."

"I know of a place," Luke said. "It's a different realm. I've only been there a couple of times." He noticed Valeen's shock. "As a visitor," he confirmed. "There are light beings there, but it was created for those that, well, need . . . more assistance than others."

Valeen stared at him openmouthed. *Oh my God, there is a world created only for the mentally unstable.* She wasn't about to say out loud what she was thinking, but she would definitely ask Luke about it later.

Luke didn't have to wait. He could tell by her expression what she was thinking. He didn't even have to probe. He could only grin at her. Slapping his thighs, he got up. "I'll go round up those horses, make sure Ian is still breathing. Maybe he could join us."

"I'll meet you out there," Tobias told him. "I think I want to check on Pip anyway," he continued as he went through the door that resembled a closet.

Luke bent down and kissed Valeen passionately. "We won't be long," he told her, hovering less than an inch above her lips. Her eyes fluttered open. She loved the way he could make her feel like she was the only person in his world with just a kiss.

"Okay, I'll wait, then," she replied playfully. He smiled, pecked her lips again, and left.

Laura came in a few minutes later, and Valeen noticed a little spring in her step that went along with her smile.

"You killed him, didn't you?"

Laura went to the coffee pot, poured herself a cup, and brought the pot with her to fill Valeen's cup. "Don't be ridiculous. I love that man. He's apparently going with Luke and Tobias to find Cornelius." She set the pot on the table and sat down. "I don't know why. Eventually the dragons would find him."

"Laura!" Valeen scolded.

Laura sighed. "Yeah, I know, that was harsh, and really, I don't think the dragons would deliberately harm him, and I know for certain he won't be causing any more harm to them."

Valeen took a sip of her coffee. "So what did you need to talk to Ian about?"

Before Laura could answer, Tobias came through the door to Pip's room. Valeen didn't have to ask—Tobias answered her question without prompting.

"Pip will be all right. You were right, he just needed some time to himself. He's drawing now."

Laura stood up. "I'll fill you in later," she told Valeen. "I think I want some of that alone time myself."

When Tobias and Laura left through separate doors, Valeen stayed seated. She topped off her cup and just sat in the quiet, contemplating her choices and what her part in the scheme of things would be. She couldn't help imagining what it would be like.

CHAPTER *Seventeen*

L uke, Tobias, and Ian returned just as the suns were setting. Even though it wouldn't get fully dark, they had called it a day. It had been a long one. Valeen and Laura had been watching for their return; Valeen was elated at the news Laura had finally shared with her and was anxious for Luke to return so she could tell him. When they saw Luke, Ian, and Tobias heading for the stables, they went out to meet them.

"Well?" Laura interrogated when the three men sauntered out.

Ian shook his head. "We found a place he might have rested through the night, but the way things are growing and changing so quickly, it was difficult to track him. We can try again tomorrow."

"Did you see any sign of Areve or the others?" Valeen asked.

Tobias looked up to the sky in wonder. "No, but I didn't expect we would. They're pretty good at camouflage."

"They could be right under our noses and we wouldn't know it, similar to owls at home. They make no sound when they fly," Luke added, searching the trees.

"Oh, oh, did Ian tell you?" Valeen asked excitedly, grabbing Luke's arm.

Luke smiled. "Yes, he told us. I think it will be good."

"Good? That's all you can say? You think it will be good?"

"Okay, it's wonderful, fantastic, amazing. What do you want from me, woman?"

Valeen realized she was acting a bit frantic at the idea and glanced at Tobias. She couldn't really read his expression; he had gone somewhere else. There seemed to be a hint of relief in his demeanor but also sadness—Valeen just wasn't sure for what. So many things had happened in the last few days. "I'm sure your dad will be fine. The man has some serious survival skills," she told him, settling on something she knew for certain could be an apparent challenge.

"Are you guys hungry? You've been gone for hours," Laura interjected, feeling the discomfort coming off Tobias.

"I could eat," Luke answered, kissing Valeen on the side of the head. "How about you two?" he asked Ian and Tobias.

"Sounds good to me," Ian agreed.

Tobias stared at the house, then at his feet. "I'm not very hungry right now. I'll get something later, but thank you." Luke nodded in understanding.

"We can put something aside for you," Valeen added, taking Luke by the hand as they turned to go inside.

They all turned back when they heard the thump and whoosh of wings behind them, startled to see the sky and trees full of dragons. Different shapes, sizes, and bright, spectacular colors exploded around them. None of them could speak. *Where did they come from?* Valeen wondered. *I didn't hear anything.*

As the last of them landed on the ground, a figure sliding off the back of one of the dragons caught their attention. Everyone froze, expecting Cornelius to come into the light.

"Hey ho!" a cheerful voice called as he scooted between two dragons, waving an arm in the air.

"Ruben?" Tobias asked in bewilderment.

"The cook?" Valeen and Laura asked simultaneously.

"Aye. It is me."

Tobias dropped his head and shoulders in relief. "What in all the hells are you doing?"

"I'm sorry, lad. I just couldn't do it anymore. I'll explain everything, I swear, but I would really like to get clean and have a decent meal now that it's relatively safe." No one moved. "I promise, Tobias, everything is good. I will explain, but I'm begging you, please let me shower. It will benefit everyone."

Tobias nodded and gestured to the house. He glanced at Areve and Praxton as he turned to follow. *Everything is all right. We'll talk more in the morning,* he heard Areve say in his mind.

Laura quickened her pace to walk with Valeen. She leaned in close and whispered, "We have been eating ham, right?" Then she let out a yelp when Valeen elbowed her in the ribs. Laura scowled at her, rubbing her side. "Geez, I was just kidding. It's been pretty intense around here."

"I know it has, but I think it's about to get even more intense. How does your brain even go there anyway?" Valeen whispered back.

Laura shrugged. "It's a gift. But really, I noticed how tense you were and just wanted to take your mind off whatever it was that had you walking like a steel bar. It worked."

Valeen smiled down at her feet. "You are the better friend. And I'm glad you're feeling like your old self again. I was beginning to worry."

Laura leaned her head back to gaze at the lavender sky as they walked. "Really, it's just another day in the life of Valeen's world."

***

They were all gathered around the table; even Pip attended, his curiosity peaked. Ruben came in looking much better, with his hair still wet and slicked back. His face was shaven, and he had on clean clothes. "Don't worry, I burned the clothes I had on," he told them humorously. When no one responded, he cleared his throat and took a seat. "Yeah, well, okay then."

Everyone looked to Tobias to take the lead; even though the curiosity was almost overwhelming as they held back their own questions, in silent agreement they waited for Tobias to ask the questions.

Ruben looked around the table at the bandaged, beaten-up, and baffled expressions of the people around the table and sighed. "I guess you're all wondering where I've been," he began.

"You said you were going for supplies," Pip told him hotly.

Ruben was surprised at his accusing tone. He had never heard Pip speak above a meek whisper to anyone. *What has happened here?* he wondered as he replayed all the events that had transpired, and continued.

"I did—I was." He stopped and exhaled heavily. "I just wanted to check on the ladies before I left."

"Ladies? What ladies?" Tobias interrupted.

"Maybe we should let him finish," Valeen said gently, touching his arm.

Tobias rubbed his eyes. "Please, Ruben, continue."

Ruben smiled at Valeen. "Thank you, ma'am. Well, I just couldn't do it. When the General told me to dispose of the females after they released their eggs, I just couldn't. So I waited until dark and led them into the trees. I don't know what it was exactly, but they seemed so sad and frightened, and I just couldn't. So I set them free." He looked around at the now-stunned expressions, and when no one responded, he continued. "I knew you were taking tender care of the little ones—" He gestured to Tobias. "—and I told the mothers as much. I don't know if they understood or not. But I did my best to explain and reassure them."

"They understood," Ian said, grinning down at his hands.

"I also know of the one you kept in the forest," Ruben went on. "But

I figured it was safer for all of us that we keep our secrets to ourselves."

Tobias nodded his agreement.

"Well, like I said, I went to check on them, and they were nowhere to be found. Being concerned, as I felt they were my responsibility, I went to search for them and found another gateway. I decided they could probably take care of themselves, being dragons and all and no longer chained up, so I thought I'd go ahead and go get the supplies we needed and get back. But when I went to step through the gateway, it closed—almost had my head floating around by itself in the void. Somehow I got turned around when I went to find the other gateway, and before I knew it, I was lost." He blew out his embarrassment through puffed cheeks, and when still no one responded, he went on. "I must have wandered around for two, maybe three days; I lost track. And, to my surprise, there were berries growing on bushes, and I found a little stream of fresh water. Did you know there was water that ran through this realm?" he suddenly asked Tobias, but didn't wait for him to answer. "Then that strange dragonfly found me. I think he stalked me for a while before he let me know he was there. Talked to me, can you believe that? I was talking to a bug!"

Everyone except Tobias grinned at the memory of their own reactions to Sabastian, then Valeen remembered what Sabastian had said. *'There are others, and another.' He must have been talking about Ruben. Not so crazy after all.*

"He led me to the rest of the tribe," Ruben went on. "They welcomed me enough—and by that, I mean they didn't try to eat me—so I just stayed with them until I came up with a plan. Then Praxton showed up, and thank goodness he could speak in a language I understood. You did well with him, Tobias. He had told me and the others what was happening here, and, well, here I am."

Tobias could only stare at Ruben in disbelief. "I had no idea how you felt," he finally said. He looked around at the people seated around the table, who were also stunned into silence. He sighed heavily, releasing the shock, and in that moment decided to let it all go. "I'm glad you're here, Ruben, and I'm happy you're safe. I've really missed your cooking." He smiled widely and chuckled at Ian's feigned expression of being offended and hurt.

"Well, I'm exhausted now," Laura announced.

"Me too," Valeen agreed. "Maybe we should all get some rest. Talk to Areve and the rest of the tribe tomorrow."

Everyone muttered their agreement as they stood up from the table.

Laura tugged on Ian's shirt and nodded toward Pip. Ian nodded back. "Pip, can Laura and I have a word?"

Pip was feeling pretty tired himself and a little sad. "Sure, I guess," he shrugged.

"Will you show me your drawings?" Laura asked enthusiastically.

"Sure," he answered solemnly, shrugging his other shoulder. "They're down in my rooms." He headed through the doorway that was not a closet (it was still disturbing to Ian).

Laura was actually surprised: Even though the room was poorly lit, it was clean and organized. She had missed the details when she came down to tuck him in the other night. There were dozens of hand-drawn and painted pictures in varying degrees of expertise. It was obvious Pip had been drawing for years, improving as he grew. She stood in front of a wall that resembled a mural of different worlds. "These are amazing, Pip," she told him, genuinely impressed.

"They're okay," Pip replied, sitting heavily on his bed.

Ian sat next to him. "Pip, me and Laura were talking about how much we enjoy your company and were wondering if you'd like to go back with us when we leave."

Pip's heart beat frantically in his chest as he remembered hoping for just that. "You mean to visit?" he asked eagerly.

Laura came to sit on the other side of him. "No, we mean for you to come and stay, to live with us, in our world. Ian has horses and a farm," she hurried on. She and Ian looked at each other over Pip's head when he just went quiet.

They want me to live with them? "You mean, like, forever?"

"Well, yes. Or until you get old enough and you want to leave," Ian answered a little nervously, not sure where this was going. His ego really hadn't thought Pip would have a doubt.

"What about Tobias? Can he come too?"

Laura chewed on her lower lip. She really shouldn't be the one to tell Pip what plans Tobias had; that should be a conversation between him and Pip. "Of course he can, if he would like to. You are both more than welcome."

Pip stayed quiet for a few more minutes. Both Ian and Laura were beginning to get anxious.

"Would I be like your son?" he finally asked.

The question threw both of them off their stride, and Laura's eyes welled with tears. She breathed them back in. "We would like that very much," she told him, glancing again at Ian, who was also holding back his emotions.

To Laura's utter surprise, in one quick movement, Pip leapt into her arms, wrapping his arms tightly around her neck. Laura looked at Ian as both their eyes glistened in the dim light. "I was hoping you wanted me to be your son," Pip mumbled into her shoulder. She closed her eyes and squeezed him tighter, letting the tears of joy fall.

CHAPTER *Eighteen*

V aleen was restless and couldn't get comfortable. She was exhausted, but her thoughts circled. *What if I can't achieve what they want? What if I'm not strong enough? What if I'm wrong? What if they don't really need us? What if now we're just overstaying our welcome and they're just politely waiting for us to leave . . . ?*

"You're going to what-if yourself into a frenzy," Luke told her groggily, his back to her.

Valeen startled. "I thought you were sleeping."

He turned over to face her. "How can I sleep with all that commotion going on in your head?"

Valeen scowled at him. "You could stay out of my head."

Luke brushed her hair over her brow. "I could, but what fun would that be?"

Valeen didn't answer. She went back to the questions and the uncertainty she was feeling.

"It will all be all right. We'll talk to them tomorrow." Luke rolled onto his back and shut his eyes. "Besides, if they wanted us gone, I'm sure we would know it by now."

Valeen also rolled onto her back and closed her eyes. "I'm sure you're right. I'm just not as sure about myself." They both went quiet, and she tried to think of something else. *I wonder how things went with Pip . . . ?*

Shush, she heard Luke say into her thoughts. Grinning in the shadows, she drifted off to sleep, where all the answers to her question revealed themselves.

***

Cornelius had found an old branch to use as a crutch to help him walk, and he stumbled upon a stream he hadn't known was ever there. He drank deeply and then washed his cuts and soaked his injured knee. He thought about making some kind of trap for the smaller woodland animals he saw frolicking through the rapidly growing brush that he couldn't remember seeing here before, but decided he didn't have the proper tools and settled for nuts and berries that he also couldn't remember being there.

He didn't hear the tribe of dragons until they were right over him. He dove under the nearest bush. *Where did they all come from?* he wondered, biting down on his panic, then froze and squeezed his eyes shut as younger ones bounded through the bushes, following on the ground. Only one stopped and sniffed at him, quickly lost interest, and ran off.

When the last was out of sight, he cautiously wiggled out from under his cover, just in case there were stragglers. "What is going on?" he asked the trees. *I have to get back to the compound. I have to get to the weapons.*

He clambered up with some difficulty, using the stick to bear his weight. He pushed the pain in his leg to the back of his mind, making it a distant awareness, and searched the sky once more. Backtracking his initial course, he turned to follow in the direction the dragons were headed.

He had been shamed and disgraced, had lost all dignity. He had failed the realms that summoned him to rid all the worlds from the savagery of these murdering beasts. His own wife and child had been their victims, and his most recent guests, who had come to admire his work. All of them—they had been enthralled and murdered. How could he face the other rulers? But now . . .

I have to kill their queen. My son, my only son, he told me. He told me what to do, but I didn't listen, and now he's dead like his mother. They killed them, killed them both. I just need to make it back to the compound, I just need my weapons. My men will be there waiting for me.

Cornelius stopped. He was out of breath and confused as he looked around. *Where am I? What is this place? How did I get here? Who brought me here . . . ? The dragons! They cast a spell. I have to get back. My wife and son are in danger! I must save them, save them all!*

***

Valeen awoke to the sound of birds chirping and the feel of sunshine beaming through the window, and for a moment she felt like she was back at home, waking from a fantastic dream. Then she opened her eyes to the royal blue atrocity of the décor in her room. She laid on her back, her arms resting on the pillow, and stared up at the ceiling through the mesh of the canopy. "Okay, not a dream," she said to the room, but as the memory of her actual dreams came to the surface, revealing the answers she needed, she smiled to herself. *Well, Val, here goes nothing.*

She started to sit up as Luke walked in. "Are you ready?" he asked.

"As ready as I'm going to be," she replied heavily.

"Good." He held up a steaming mug and grinned. "I have coffee."

When they entered the kitchen, they were greeted with smiling faces. Valeen looked over to Laura and Ian. They were beaming like the proud new parents they were, as was Pip, who all but glowed.

"Good morning," Valeen said to the room.

Laura took a bit of toast and nodded toward her. "You overslept, almost missed breakfast."

Valeen made her way to an empty chair with her coffee. "It's okay. I don't think I'm very hungry anyway," she sighed.

"Did you hear?" Pip asked with proud excitement. "Tobias is going to be a traveler," he hurried on, not waiting for Valeen to answer. "He's going to all the realms ever, and telling them about the dragons, the truth about them. Ruben is going with him, and I get to go live with Laura and Ian and the horses. Rosy gets to go with us!" he elaborated enthusiastically. "I'll be their son," he boasted further, giving a short nod of satisfaction.

Valeen was astonished at the transformation in this young boy in so little time. "That is wonderful news, all of it," she replied, barely containing her own excitement.

Tobias and Ruben came in through the kitchen door, Ruben grinning like a fool. It was a contagious grin, and Valeen noticed immediately the lighter steps in Tobias's walk, a genuine ease to his movements. *Yep, this really has been an amazing adventure. Who knew?*

Sabastian buzzed in behind them just as Tobias was about to close the door. "It is time, yes, yes, it—oooh, neat inside, yes—no! Hot, too hot." He flew to the window and bumped against it several times. "Out, out, please. Out, pleeease."

Tobias went to the window and gently gathered Sabastian up in his hands. "It's all right, Sabastian. I'll take you out, but what were you going to tell us?"

Sabastian settled in the palm of his hand. "Thank you, Thank you, yes." He looked around at the people seated around the table, then around at his surroundings. "Yes, yes. Neat inside!"

"Sabastian," Tobias said firmly.

It was obvious Sabastian was feeling the same excitement as everyone else. The difference was that he probably knew more than any of them. "Yes, it is time, it is. It is time, yes. Areve said tribe is ready, yes, they are. They are ready. Neat inside, yes, but hot! Let me out, please, please."

Tobias smiled down at the dragonfly pleadingly staring up at him and went to the door. "Of course, thank you, Sabastian."

When he opened the door, Sabastian immediately flew out but hovered in the threshold. "Yes, very neat, not staying," he said, and flew away.

Pip giggled. "He's funny."

Ian mussed Pip's hair, the sound of his laughter echoing in his heart. "Yes, he is."

Ruben shook his head and went to the sink to wash up. "Strange little insect," he mumbled.

"So, what, do we just go outside and wait for instruction?" Laura asked.

Luke stood and held out his hand for Valeen to take. "I guess so. Are you ready?"

Valeen put her hand in Luke's and let him pull her up. "As ever I will be. Shall we?" she said, gesturing toward the door.

They all gathered in the center of the compound just outside Lixten's old lair. They watched in fascination as the dragons appeared out of the trees, their colors changing like chameleons right before their eyes. *That's how they do that,* Valeen thought with admiration. *What amazing beings.*

Areve and Lixten moved forward. "Thank you for this," Areve told Valeen. "It is a special kind of being that allows themselves to be an instrument of such power."

Areve's words were sincere and meaningful, but Valeen was still hoping she was the right person for the job.

"You are," Lixten rumbled.

Valeen blushed, forgetting they also had that little gift of hearing her thoughts.

Lixten bent down to be nose to nose with Valeen. "I trust the Winged Gods to know what is best for us," he told her.

Valeen had no words. She was feeling a little intimidated, not just by Lixten's silent stare, as if he were probing her soul, but also by being face to face with such an enormous, powerful being.

"We trust you," he told her. "I trust you."

This last statement put her at ease, but she could only nod her acknowledgment.

Areve silently took a few steps back, as did the other dragons. Valeen noticed Mara and Praxton standing off to one side. She glanced back at Luke, who nodded his support, and stepped forward.

As Valeen approached Lixten, she felt a little apprehensive. Even though she'd been shown what do in her dreams, she wasn't entirely sure how it would work out. But as she laid her hands along the scar on Lixten's neck, she felt the pull of energy. Then a surge of heat flashed through her body. Her thoughts became fuzzy, and bursts of color erupted behind her closed eyes. She allowed the powers that be to use her as a conduit. In her mind's eye she saw the golden spirals weave their way up from the scar on Lixten's neck, moving and connecting through intricate designs embedded in the individual scales of his entire body.

Luke stood next to Tobias, and when he saw Valeen's body go rigid, he instinctively took a step forward, only to be stopped by Tobias, who gently grabbed his arm to keep him back. Luke scowled at him, but when Sabastian reverently landed on his shoulder and grinned, he knew he was right to stay back. He needed to trust her.

Laura, Ian, and Pip stood together, watching in fascination the gold and silver starbursts spreading out on Lixten and the others as they formed a half-circle around him and Valeen. Ruben stood on the other side of Tobias, hands in his pockets, leaning back on his heels and smiling widely, just like Luke did when he was supremely satisfied.

Then the music came. Laura imagined several thousand horns and violins playing all at once. The vibration in the air, at first, had the leaves on the trees and shrubs shimmering and shaking in the wake of the sound. Then the ground began to tremble, quaking buildings and rattling equipment loose, knocking one of bolts stacked against the barn onto the ground. As it got louder, Ian wrapped his arms tighter around Laura and Pip, but closed his eyes and let the music play in his mind.

The windows in the house exploded, sending tiny shards of glass out into the painted yard. They all instinctively ducked their heads, even though they were not close enough to the house to be harmed. Pip covered his ears but was smiling, enjoying the spectacular show. Tobias was in complete awe of the breathtaking display of power and love, taking mental notes to record in his journals. He let the rush of energy flow freely through him and, like Ian, closed his eyes and listened to the glorious song of a dragon's tribe as it vibrated through his heart and mind.

***

Cornelius watched them from the trees. He had stuffed leafy branches and shrubs in his clothes and painted mud on his face, trying to blend in with the scenery. His heart pounded in his chest, he was sweating, and a vein in his temple throbbed. *What are they doing? This is madness! I must stop it. The ghosts are there—what if they don't die?* His fractured mind reeled in circles. *Ghosts don't bleed,* a distant voice in the back of his mind echoed, but he dismissed it. He was about to witness some kind of evil ceremony. *I have to stay alert. I have to be ready.*

He watched in horror as the dragons' colors changed, as they all went into some kind of trance. *This is my chance. I've got to get to the catapult while everyone is distracted.* Then the noise came, and he took it as a sign.

He made his way through the trees, sneaking behind the line of dragons. He spotted the bolt lying next to the machine and the dangling chains just above it. *I could make it.* Focused on the weapons, he moved as quickly as he could. He jumped and tripped, falling to the ground when the windows of his house blew out. The noise was deafening, rattling his bones.

As he stood, his body felt like it was moving through molasses. Forcing his body to move, he managed to get the chains around the bolt. Using the pulley system attached to the weapon, he maneuvered it into place. He didn't have the strength in his legs to pedal the catapult to a safer distance from the barn, but he could use the hand cranks to swing the bolt into position.

Valeen started to feel like she was being brought out of a dream as the magic began to withdraw. She felt exhilarated, refreshed—she felt alive! She couldn't help the giggle that bubbled out of her throat as she slowly pulled her hands away from Lixten.

Lixten turned to look down at her. She wasn't sure if she should say something or wait for him to, but before the question could fully form in her mind, Lixten lifted his head and fire erupted into the sky.

Luke started to go to Valeen but stopped abruptly, shielding his face when Lixten let loose his fire. At first it was a hot blue flame, filled with years of resentment and shame, then the color changed to yellow, streaked with bright blues and greens. *Even their fire is different from one another,* Luke thought.

Sabastian hopped up and down on Luke's shoulder, chanting excitedly, "Yes! Yes! My prince has his fire! He does, he does have it."

Mara was tugged out of the energy field when something caught her attention. It was a faint, familiar scent. She lifted her head to sniff the air. *The General!* She swung around, searching the grounds, and spotted him sitting in the seat of that hideous contraption, cranking a handle that moved the bolt toward her tribe.

Areve and Praxton, being the closest to her, heard her thoughts first. Praxton didn't understand, but the sudden panic he felt was real. Before Areve could respond, Mara had moved like lightning and was standing atop the bolt, talons digging in she glared down at Cornelius, baring razor-sharp teeth.

"Mara, no!" Tobias screamed as he ran toward the catapult. "Mara, please wait!"

She doesn't understand what you're saying, Ian's voice echoed in his thoughts.

Tobias, wait! It was Areve's voice.

Tobias was out of breath. He held on to the side of the machine, leaning over to catch his breath. He looked up at Cornelius, who was frozen in terror, unable to look away from Mara's teeth, inches from his face.

Mara, please, Tobias begged.

Mara, this is not our way, Areve calmly stated as she approached Mara from behind. *Trocaire, Mara.* Mara glanced at Areve and back at Cornelius, leaning even closer to his face. Areve moved in closer to Mara. *Maithius, that is our way.*

Lixten, Praxton, and the other dragons gathered around Areve, while Ian, Luke, and the other people gathered around Tobias. Ian leaned in to Tobias and whispered, "What is she saying? I don't know those words."

Tobias grinned in spite of the circumstances and whispered back. "She is telling her to have mercy and forgiveness."

Ruben laid a hand on Tobias's shoulder, trying to give some comfort to a situation that had just turned real bad real fast. He felt completely helpless, even though he understood the rage he saw in Mara.

Lixten came up beside Mara, nudging her chin with his snout. *He is not worth it. Tobias is going to go tell the other realms, explain our ways. This is not our way. This human is no threat to us any longer. Don't make it so Tobias has to tell untruths.*

Mara looked down at Tobias's worried expression, filled with something she didn't understand. *He is my father,* he told her with regretful eagerness.

Mara looked back at Cornelius. His eyes darted around at the dragons and people who had him surrounded, then back at Mara. She leaned in, hitting him in the forehead with her snout and knocking him out of his seat onto the ground. She yanked the bolt from the catapult, snapping chains as she did, and carried it off into the trees. It seemed the whole realm exhaled with relief.

Tobias and Ian helped Cornelius to his feet, and Luke had found some rope to tie him.

"They are murderers. I saw. Ghosts don't bleed." Cornelius looked at Tobias, confused and wild-eyed. "They killed you, they murdered my sweet Heather. Ghosts don't bleed." He looked around at the other sad faces. "They killed all of you."

Luke tightened the rope around Cornelius's wrists and glanced at Valeen, who was wrapped around Laura and Pip, sad pity etched on their faces as Cornelius didn't struggle or fight, just stood babbling nonsense.

"They killed you, they killed me" were the last words Cornelius spoke before going silent and retreating to somewhere in his broken mind.

Luke looked at Tobias. "The gateways are open."

Tobias nodded and glanced at Pip, who looked frightened. "We'll take care of him," he reassured. "Let's go, then," he told Luke.

Luke walked over to Valeen and kissed her. "We'll be back shortly."

As they led Cornelius away, the dragons also turned away and began to blend into the trees, giving them all time to realign their emotions.

Sabastian sat on Areve's back with his head hung. "Yes, sad, so sad" was all even he could say.

Valeen and the others started to walk away when Valeen had a thought. "Wait, what about Mara? We didn't heal her fire."

Areve turned around and smiled at her. "Yes, we did," she told her, turning and walking into trees, fading into the scenery.

Sabastian, who was still unusually somber, flew down from Areve and hovered in front of Valeen. "Heal one, heal all. Yes, yes." He bumped Valeen's nose and flew away, following the dragons into the trees.

Valeen stood blinking in surprise at Sabastian's gentle poke and his and Areve's words. Surrendering, she shook her head and joined the others, who had begun to saunter toward the windowless house in silence, broken glass crunching under their feet. She startled and turned around quickly when something shoved her from behind. It was Lixten she was face to face with, making her breath hitch.

"Thank you," he rumbled.

Valeen was not in a state to be cordial. "I'd like to say 'anytime,' but . . . well." She looked around and shrugged. "Your home is beautiful, and maybe we'll come back to visit. So, for now, you're welcome."

Lixten smiled at her, showing his sharp teeth, then turned to follow the others into the trees.

Luke and Ian returned within the hour. Tobias looked sad but relieved. Valeen and Laura had everything packed, and Ian had helped Pip gather his belongings, tying them onto Rosy's back. They walked Rosy to the gateway entrance, where she waited knowingly for them to return. They now all sat around the table for their goodbyes.

"Ruben will be going with me to the other realms. He will be my witness to what happened here," Tobias stated. He looked warmly at Pip. "You'll be in good hands." He smiled at Laura and Ian.

"I know I'll be," Pip answered, grinning up at Ian. "Are we ready to go?" he asked eagerly.

"We are," Luke said, and they all stood up and made their way to the gateway.

EPILOGUE

Valeen felt a familiar peace and enlightenment flow subtly into her heart as she knelt in front of freshly planted flowers. She looked down at her hands, covered in rich, cool dirt. She envisioned a sparkling energy moving through her whole being and realized it didn't feel as odd or unnatural as it used to. She thought of Zurry and Fioria, the gnome and fairy, and how those magical beings had played such a huge role in her awakening.

"We create and expand as we go," she remembered Emery telling her when she had traveled to the Uncreated Place, and she thought of Sabastian, unconsciously making her smile. And all of a sudden, everything felt incredibly right. It was in this moment that Valeen became aware of exactly who she was, who they all were. There wasn't an inkling of fear or doubt. Everything became very clear to her.

This is who I am. This is the magic in my world. What a fantastic gift. Any need to understand was gone. It just was.

As she knelt on the ground in front of her flowers, taking in all the beauty around her, a large winged shadow flew above her. She sat back on her heels and closed her eyes, tilting her head for the warmth of sun to fall upon her face.

She inhaled deeply. "Okay, what's next?"

ABOUT THE AUTHOR

Kathleen Bradford lives in the urban valleys of Utah with her husband of twenty years and their Shih Tzu, Bear. She is a writer of multi-dimensional beauty and has been composing and writing stories since she was in grade school—writing pen to paper, unknowing what will happen on the next page, transcribing hundreds of pages into a Microsoft Word document.

Inspired by her own experiences, profound observations, and a vast imagination, she developed an abstract view of the world which is reflected in stories that captivate young and old alike.

When she was young, Kathleen wanted to be an astronaut, but life's events guided her to work with and care for children, experiencing the world by seeing it through their eyes—watching and learning while encouraging and embracing their different ideas and visions. She now works as an accountant by day and remains an enthusiastic stargazer, thoroughly enjoying and studying every aspect of nature's beauty and complexity.

Her greatest passions are creating new adventures and bringing them to life in the written word, and connecting with her family and her "tribe" as often as possible.

ABOUT THE PUBLISHER

Glass Spider Publishing is a hybrid micropublisher located in Ogden, Utah. The company was founded in 2016 by writer Vince Font to help authors get their works into shape, into print, and into distribution. Visit www.glassspiderpublishing.com to learn more.